A
Destiny
in
Sapphire

Jessica Florence

Editing by Magnifico Manuscripts

Proofreading by Virginia Tesi Carey

Cover by Sarah Hansen, Okay Creations©

Chapter One

Sapphira

Anyone who thought my power was the greatest in the world could suck it. Yes, I was a Fae princess with the power of absorption. After touching someone, I collected a little bit of their magic to keep forever. But I could only use it for a length of time before the power needed to replenish.

My father had dual cores of onyx and a dragon, so shifting was effortless for him. I'd been raised by Verin and only found out that Desmire was my father shortly before I took out my core. My memories disappeared, and I became human. But ever since I was reunited with my sapphire core, all the powers of people I'd touched came rushing back, and I hadn't known what to do with them.

Becoming a dragon like my father was harder than I could have imagined. I'd managed to lift off the ground only to face-plant into the sand seconds later. Since my dad had the essence, I had hoped I would have some natural instinct in my blood to become the beast. However, after an hour of jumping and flapping my large membranous wings, I crashed to the ground and in Fae form. I'd even tried to change into an owl like Dris, thanks to some of her powers I'd absorbed, but failed miserably. Sand flew into my mouth, and I cursed violently. The sun had grown closer to the dunes, and I assumed dusk was near.

I wish Lethirya had touched my skin, then I'd be able to portal home right away. Sadly, she was meticulous in her capture of me . . . no contact that transferred power.

I climbed to my feet and walked west. Hopefully I'd find some shelter or a village. I wished I knew where I was besides the desert. I'd studied maps as a Fae princess and examined human globes during my human years. Mongolia had a desert like this, but so did Africa, Australia, and Peru on the human globe. The Fae realm hosted many deserts I'd yet to visit on the opposite side of the world. Usually their geography mirrored each other. Crysia was very much like Yosemite National Park, where the portal to cross realms stood.

Slowly, I trudged to the top of the nearest dune.

"More desert." I sighed. No buildings or villages as far as I could see in any direction. I noticed some white rock but needed to wait until sunset before attempting to reach it. Random bushes scattered across the landscape. Maybe I could lie beneath it for shade until the sun set. I'd have to create a shelter of some kind to rest. I needed sleep. My body felt weary, and the powers within had to replenish. Slowly, I walked toward the grouping of bushes toward the bottom of the dune.

There wasn't much shade, but it was better than nothing. I dropped to my knees and cursed. Everything ached, and I prayed no creature lurked in the desired shade.

"If someone is there, make some room!" I hollered at the bushes and waited for something to slither or jump out. Nothing did, so I pushed the lower dry branches up, then crawled beneath them. It took a little bit of wiggling, but I managed to settle between the scratchy bush and the sand. A let out a deep breath as I attempted to relax my frustrated mind. No good decisions came from an overstimulated brain.

"OK, Sapphira, we are lost in the desert. Now what?" I asked myself and waited for the wind or my conscience to whisper the answers to my dilemma. Unfortunately, neither had an answer. Food, shelter, and water were the biggest priorities. I'd been in battle before my pyscho cousin, Lethirya, had kidnapped and abandoned me. Verin had wanted me out of the way. He wouldn't kill me, but he'd leave me to die via harsh elements.

I missed my home, my mate Rune, and my friends. A smile crossed my lips as I remembered the sight of my mother and father flying in to save us from the Dramens, thus winning the battle at Crystoria.

With magic flowing through the Fae lands once again, my mother was back to her normal self. No more riddles or incoherent murmurs. My strong mother, the warrior, the Queen of Crysia had returned.

"What a mess." Tears burst from my eyes as I thought of my loved ones' faces. I hoped they were OK. Rune was probably going insane after watching Lethirya pull me through a portal. I hoped my mother calmed him from destroying everything we had fought to save. So much had happened in such a short time. I had to roll with it while my mind fought to catch up to reality. Just as I thought of reality, a little flutter tickled the inside of my belly. More tears came as I recognized that flutter came from the baby growing there.

From what I remember, Fae and human pregnancies were different. Humans carried the babe for nine months before birth. The Fae only carried for about three months. Fae children also grew quickly before settling into immortality. Having a healer look over me would be a first step once I reached Crysia. Until then, I closed my eyes and willed myself to breathe deeply.

When you feel lost and not sure what to do, you focus on the next step.

My next step was to breathe, and after that I'd take another deep breath. I waited in the spotty shade of the bush until the sun had fallen behind the dune. My body craved sustenance but I couldn't find any nearby. I inched out from the bush and searched for the white rock I'd seen earlier. If I could make it there, I'd have a chance at a shelter. I didn't know what sort of animals came out at night to hunt in this terrain. I thought about transforming into a dragon again, but when I pulled at the power, it didn't come. It still needed time. If only I had access to food and water, that would accelerate the process. As I raced toward the rocks with my Fae speed, I scanned the sand for anything to eat.

Surprisingly, I made it to the large rock after thirty minutes of running up and down the cursed dunes. I gasped as my lungs heaved air in and out . . . too much activity for one day. My body and mind were drained. Still, I needed shelter. With one last push of my powers, I pulled at the rock, and wall-like planks rose. With great effort, I piled them into a makeshift shelter. It would have to do for the night. The rock would block the wind or any sandstorms that crept my way, and the stone-like house would protect me from creatures. I slumped into my new temporary home and closed the rock door. Bits of moonlight snuck through the cracks, and I placed a hand on my stomach.

"Good night, little one. Tomorrow, we will come up with a plan to get home. Your daddy is probably going nuts without us."

Chapter Two

Rune

"The border is active but nothing has gotten past our guards yet." Najen bowed his head at the queen on the dais.

"Still ripple backs?" Olyndria pursed her lips as Najen nodded. Verin had been sending vile monsters to test our borders for weaknesses since we had arrived back in Crysia.

"General Rune, any new information from our scouts?" All heads in the room turned to me, and I shook my head. My wolf and my heart would have known if Sapphira was dead. Scouts were sent in all directions of the continent to find her. Nothing yet, and it pissed me off. It'd been two days since she was taken from me. I'd become a vessel of silent rage. My essence begged me to shed my skin and become the beast to hunt for her. However, as the general of Crysia's armies, I had to make sure our kingdom was ready for war. Sapphira would smack me if I left the people to find her. She would find a way back to me. I just had to make sure she had somewhere to come back to.

"All right then. Meeting adjourned." The queen ended the meeting, and my head soldiers went back to their stations.

"How are you holding up, Rune?"

The woman sitting on the throne beckoned me closer. She'd become like a mother to me over the years. She knew Sapphira and I were mates and not only did she approve, she delighted in that knowledge. I didn't answer. I knew I hadn't been easy to be around since my mate had disappeared. I either barked or cursed at people, so I chose silence in order to keep some semblance of peace.

"I assumed no changes, but you can't fault me for asking. My daughter is strong, and I know we will find her if she doesn't find us first." The queen smiled, and my shoulders dropped an inch. Back to her normal self again, the woman had taken up her role with a vengeance. A tall warrior with brown skin and hair that mirrored my mate's walked onto the dais. Desmire. He'd tried to get me to talk to him and train to burn some of the steam out of my pores. Only I didn't feel like it. A dragon against a wolf would be a vicious fight. He looked at his queen with every ounce of love beaming through his gray eyes.

"You may go." She dismissed me, her hand reaching up to caress the warrior's hand that cupped her cheek. He didn't care for formalities. His head leaned down and kissed her despite the company. The dragon rumbled a warning and my beast understood it loud and clear. *Get out of the room and give them privacy.* I instructed the two guards at the door to find something to do for a while.

The winter air bit into the skin of my hands as I walked outside the palace. In the distance, I saw Tor and Nyx walking up the path from town, and I steered myself the other way. I liked they had each other; their opposite personalities complemented them well. However, that didn't mean I wasn't envious they had the chance to bask in the newness of their mating. Sapphira and I hadn't gotten the chance to settle into our relationship. From the beginning, it'd been a rocky path, with a few precious moments of bliss that made my heart hurt to think about. I missed her with every thunderous beat of my heart. Every moment away from her and our babe felt like someone had ripped a part of my soul from my chest. It ached, like before. Only this time I knew she wasn't trapped in onyx but whisked beyond my sight. I scanned my surroundings, then nodded to guards as I passed by only to stand in front of Celestine's cave. The spirit of the seer hadn't shown herself since we arrived. There were no whispers on the wind as I walked past the stone walls into the clearing where her little fire usually crackled.

"Celestine," I growled. My throat ached from the harsh tone. No response greeted me. I wanted to hear from the seer that my mate was safe. I knew I'd find her, one way or another. However, I refused to wait another twenty years to see Sapphira again. Screw it! If the spirit woman couldn't help me, then I'd

12

try to speak to my mate on this hallowed ground myself. I'd heard in stories throughout my life that mates connected with each other through their bond. I didn't know if it was true but worth a try.

Slowly, I lowered my body beside the fire pit and struck the flint from my pocket together over the wood inside. A small ember appeared, and I tended it into a hearty blaze. With my legs crossed beneath me, I allowed my eyes to close and my walls to come down. The wind kicked up around me, and the fire's tendrils twisted in response. I'd taught myself to quiet my mind on the eve of my first battle. The nerves of fighting and possibly dying brought warriors older than I was to their knees. Stressing about the future didn't help the outcome. I failed at giving up control many times. Right now, there wasn't shit I could do besides head to the badlands and demand Verin give me Sapphira.

I smirked at the thought, as did my inner wolf.

The wind slowed, and I focused on the fire eating at the wood. Scents of burning hickory and ash danced in the air. With each deep breath, I retreated into myself, past my tiger's eye core and my silent wolf. The beast wanted to reach his mate as much as I did. I thought of her mischievous smile and the way her eyes narrowed when she didn't know if she wanted to kiss me or fight me more. I concentrated on the gentle beating of the life growing insider her, a purpose to be better than we used to be. I had to keep my rage together for that babe. I refused to give up hope. Sitting there for minutes, hours, I quieted every sound within me to hear my woman from wherever she was. I believed in our bond . . . it survived years of separation, the loss of her sapphire core, and her broken memories.

"That snake tasted gross but it's food. We're OK, little one, everything is gonna be OK." Sapphira's voice whispered through my head, and my eyes shot open. I heard her, like the gentle breeze that rustled against my cloak. Her encouragement to our child wisped into my thoughts, then left.

My family was safe.

I sat there and tried again for hours, but her voice didn't whisper in my head again. Once was enough, though. I had to find her. I wouldn't sit and wait. I thought I could be calm and patient, but I couldn't. I would rip the earth from beneath Verin's feet until he gave me back my mate, my wife, my queen.

Chapter Three

Sapphira

I'd managed to survive another three days off cactus water and a ten-foot snake that jumped out of the dune to eat me. I was still in the Fae realm since there wasn't any orange and black snakes with little wings that I knew of in the human one. I skinned the creature with a rock I'd fashioned into a weapon and cooked it over a fire.

Twice I transformed into my dragon self but only once did I manage to get some airtime. My spirits were up; I fed the baby and myself. All in all, I managed to calm my frustrations for now. There were no humans in sight, and whatever creatures lurked about kept their distance. The baby kept me company, and I talked to the babe constantly to keep myself from going crazy. I still hadn't learned my location. However, in my dragon form, I sensed a change in the air, like water rested to the east based on the moisture in the wind. I trekked that way on foot and camped at night. The dry desert bushes were my friend during the brightest parts of the day, and I covered the most ground in the early mornings and evenings. Cold wind brushed me most of the time;

winter had settled in the air. I used my fire to keep warm when I could. Reserving magic became a priority unless I deemed using it necessary.

After five hours of walking, I decided it was time to become a dragon again. My body still wasn't used to the change, so the pain brought me to my knees in the sand. Every inch of my skin ripped apart. My bones shattered as they grew and grew until I was human no more. My blue scales shimmered in the early morning sun as I stretched my large membranous onyx-and-sapphire-colored wings. Every tiny particle of sand came into clear focus. I flapped once, then again. The sand swirled like a desert storm around me. I bent my legs to gracefully launch for the sky. Taking off wasn't my problem. It was the leveling off part I had trouble with. The giant dragon body was awkward and unfamiliar to me. Add in the large wings with a swishing tail, and I looked like a wiggling worm in the air.

"This time we're gonna do this." I mentally spoke to the babe and pushed off. Long fluid movements lifted us to the sky, and I tried hard to keep my tail straight as we inched off the ground. My tail was my stabilizer, and I repeated the pattern of flapping in my head for my wings to move in unison. Higher and higher I rose. I roared in triumph that I hadn't fallen yet and thrusted my head forward. My body sailed through the sky as I soared to what I hoped was a body of water ahead. I loved the feel of the wind against my scales, the power of my wings pushing me forward. The ground beneath me dashed by as I raced below two clouds. I was doing it! I was flying as a fucking dragon!

Gliding through the air, my vision narrowed on a shiny surface. I pushed myself a little harder and the closer I got, the water I searched for came into view. I roared then fire blasted from my snout on accident. I flew straight through the warmth, though it didn't burn. I really needed to work on controlling my dragon self. There were tan cliffs as I flew over the water and wondered if this was a great ocean between continents. If it was, that would be unfortunate. I'd grow tired and change back into a tired Fae while flying over open waters. When my wings trembled slightly, I tried to see land in the distance but only white-capped waves greeted me. Shit. I shifted my neck to the side and turned my wings, thus my direction. I had no choice but to retreat to land. Despite my tired wings, I pushed a little farther to see if there were any villages or camps nearby.

As a dragon, I covered miles within minutes. A town appeared about two miles north. Quickly, I drifted to the ground and shifted back to my Fae self while biting back the pain-filled groans. My muscles ached like I'd worked out all day. My legs cramped twice as I walked toward the smallish town of brown-and-white buildings.

"Hello!" I called out, not thinking, and then cursed myself. This town could be filled with Dramens or other enemies and I had just announced my presence. As I stepped past the first concrete building with open round windows, I heard a noise. My fingers wrapped around my stone weapon, and I steadied my weary legs for an attack.

"I am a hungry, pregnant Fae. You do not want to fuck with me right now," I warned. I searched for the source of the noise. A crashing noise and squeak echoed from the second building ahead. No one charged me, and there wasn't movement in the other buildings. On cautious feet, I tiptoed to the building as the noises intensified.

"Ah!" I kicked open the door and lit a fireball in my free hand. Dirt covered the concrete walls and the furniture. The house appeared to be deserted, with eerie similarities to the homes I had passed while traveling before. Dramens could be nearby, and this might be a trap. A chair fell over and a scuffling sound echoed around the room. My fire flared for light, and I saw two small eyes staring at me from behind the fallen chair.

"Little creature . . . are you a good creature or a bad one?" I asked and lowered myself down to see it better.

"I won't hurt you if you don't try to hurt me." I dropped my stone weapon but kept my fire burning. My skin tightened and hardened like a diamond, just in case it attacked. The animal stepped into the light, and my heart melted. It was a tiny boar with something reflecting the light on its furry back. The cute little snout wiggled as it eyed me cautiously.

"It's OK," I cooed softly.

Quicker than I would have thought, it took off and darted between my legs then out the building. I peered into the rest of the house, then moved to the other structures. No one lived here. The emptiness of each room made me feel more isolated than in the desert. With a long sigh, I gathered what materials I could into a makeshift bag and left the desolate town. It wasn't safe for me to linger around despite the shelter. When my legs couldn't take anymore, I made a rock hut near the cliffs at my back. I flicked a small fire to warm on a bundle of sticks with my chilled fingers and ate a handful of snake jerky.

"Well, it was a good day, little one. I flew in the clouds and got some supplies, like this pillow and old, smelly blanket." It felt silly to talk to a baby that couldn't talk back. But I needed someone to talk to or I'd go crazy. I had to keep my mind sharp to go home. Movement caught my attention to the right. My hand gripped a weapon, and I narrowed my sight on a little bush. Seconds later a little furry head peered to the side, and I released my tight grip. The little creature had followed me.

"Do you want some food?" I held out the meat, then grabbed a purple root I'd been debating on trying. The little pig-like snout wiggled and it took a step closer. It wasn't much bigger than a small house cat.

"Here. I don't have much, but if you're hungry you can have some." I grabbed the only plate from my bag and set it on the ground with the food on it. Hopefully, this cute creature wouldn't become something dangerous. My gut suggested it was friendly and needy. Its little hooves clicked on the rocky ground as it slowly treaded over. Eyes darted between me and the food.

"Are you all alone?" I looked around to see if there were others like it but saw none. As it cautiously grew closer, I examined the boar's unique features. Sand-colored fur, a pig-like body with two, small, pointed tusks, and a dusting of what looked like crystals on its back. Its red eyes were unnerving, but I wasn't going to judge.

"I'm alone, too," I admitted to the beast, and its head dipped down to sniff the meat, then the root.

"Take what you want." It eyed me while tiny teeth bit the root. Just as I was about to say it made a good choice, the creature hauled ass again. It took the food and didn't even nod a thanks.

"Rude."

Chapter Four

Dris

"He still isn't talking to anyone, is he?" Nyx leaned over to whisper in my ear. I shook my head as we watched Rune stomp through the garden from her suite window. Her room was in the same wing as mine near the royal floor.

"I think he is practicing the saying that if you can't say anything nice, then don't say anything at all." Sympathy pulled at my heart for the general. We still had no leads on his mate taken from battle. I'd searched through all the books for a layout of Verin's palace in the badlands, hopefully there were some accounts of his dungeons or places he may hide our princess. But Verin likely destroyed such evidence while he was king.

"I miss her." Nyx sighed, and my head shifted downward. We all did.

"We'll see her soon." I forced a smile and nudged my friend's shoulder. Despite the threat of darkness surrounding us, we still had hope. That's all we needed to make a difference. In all my favorite books, the hero faced challenges where they wished to give up. Desperation seeped off the page, and I had feared that they would give in and evil would win.

Many times, I was even tempted to skip to the end of the book to see what happened, to know the journey was worth it in the end, where everyone had a happily ever after. Then I stopped myself. The journey was what made the ending beautiful. Throughout the story, I had never lost hope the characters would push through to their best ending.

Sapphira was like the heroine in a book, and we were the readers. We had to believe she would face her trials and in the end would be crowned queen while we cried happy tears. When you believed in something, you gave it power. I hoped my belief in her made her feel stronger, wherever she was.

"I think I've cleaned her suite by hand over twenty times since we got back," Nyx admitted and I knew the reason behind her actions. She felt like she had no control over the situation with our princess's disappearance, so she cleaned as a way to gain a little control back.

"I've reorganized the land and water animal classification books twice. I've got this pent-up energy to do something, especially after our journey and the battling." I laughed, then continued to bare my thoughts.

"I love my library, but now it feels too quiet."

"I get it."

"How's it going with Emrys?" She changed the subject, and I blushed.

"We're taking things slow. I still go back and forth between wanting to kiss him or smack him, especially now that he has his powers back. He'll silently walk beside me, then talk when I am really absentminded. Makes me scream every time. Then he leaves flowers in the library every morning for me." I loved seeing the beautiful varieties he chose.

'That's sweet."

"Yeah," I agreed but didn't mention that he was also using the flowers as a puzzle for me. Flowers had meanings, and he picked them specifically to challenge me to know the meanings. I hadn't admitted it out loud to anyone. It felt like our little secret language, and I loved he not only found my mind attractive but sought to connect with me through knowledge. Sort of like foreplay of the brain. He wasn't the idiot jokester I first assumed him to be. He cared so much for our group . . . for me. He used humor as a way to make the ones he loved smile, but he would tear apart anyone who threatened our happiness. Every day I watched him and he still surprised me. He lived life like a game, and I was addicted to playing with him.

"How are you and Tor?" It was my turn to ask, and Nyx smiled sheepishly. She pushed a stray strand of her purple hair behind her ear and looked into the room. I wasn't sure I wanted to know what pleasant memories they shared in this space.

"We're good. Taking things slow, as well. Sort of a physical thing for now, but we are trying to spend as much time as we can learning about each other. The real us, ya know? I think if I ever meet his and Rune's dad, I might punch him. The guy is an asshole." She chuckled, which made me laugh. I'd heard the stories about the King of Regno Dei Lupi. He feared Rune more than any enemy, his own son. Tor was the heir to the throne, and if things went well with Nyx and his mating, then she'd be the future queen of his kingdom. It would be fun to watch their relationship unfold. A much easier plot to grasp than the one we were in now, with Verin taking his final stand, gathering forces to attack us. Whispers on the wind told of an alliance between the surviving Dramens and the evil king.

"I think I'm gonna head to bed. The queen invited us to tea bright and early before her meetings." Nyx stood and I popped up after her. Normally I slept like a dead person, but ever since our journey, I'd struggled. We hugged goodbye and I left her room for mine. The scents of orange and cinnamon from my dried bowl of potpourri greeted me after opening the door, and I smiled. Nothing like the scents of my youth to welcome me home. I liked my room simple and organized like the library. I had art hanging on the wall from my favorite artisans in town. Three bookshelves lined the wall by the window seat that I favored reading in every morning. I could watch the sun rise with a cup of tea and a book. My light-blue bed and comforter beckoned me, but I needed a bath first.

Twenty minutes later, I was naked and slowly climbing into my stone tub to soak. My muscles still ached from the battle against the Dramens. I was not used to being such a warrior, and it showed. I'd asked Emrys to work with me on fighting skills, and he obliged. I barely survived. With the upcoming war, I needed to do better. The breeze drifted through the open window of my room and twirled around my silvery hair.

"She's aliveeee," it whispered, and I sighed heavily. Birds knew the language of the wind and its secrets. Being an owl Fae gave me that access. For days, I'd asked the wind for clues on Sapphira with no replies. She must be far away for it to take this long to receive an answer. I'd have to tell the group my suspicions. My body grew agitated in the water, so I ended my bath earlier than normal and dried off.

I loved fashion and splurged on unique outfits whenever I could. My nighttime clothes were some of my favorites. I didn't need a man to tell me about my beauty. I wore the sexy negligees for myself. My soft bed greeted me, and I snuggled in. Hopefully, I'd fall asleep then dream blissfully. Hours passed, and I tossed and turned in bed constantly. Finally, I gave up and lit a few of my favorite scented candles, then grabbed a book. If I couldn't dream, then I'd lose myself in the written word.

A soft knock on my door snagged my attention, and I quickly fastened a robe on to answer the door.

Chapter Five

Emrys

I couldn't sleep and thought I'd bother Dris by stopping by. She liked it when I surprised her, and I wanted to please.

"It's you." She tightened her knee-length blue robe at the sight of me, and I slid into her room.

"Couldn't sleep and figured I'd come over for reading time." I assumed she would be up, since she hadn't been sleeping well since we had returned to Crysia. The candles and open book by the bed confirmed my suspicions.

"This isn't a children's reading circle." She held the door open, and I strode over to her bed and plopped down. She sighed, her eyes staring at the ceiling. It was a game we played where she pretended she didn't want me around but in reality, she liked my company. Slowly, she closed the door and walked over to me, her hands tight across her chest.

"Come over here and read me a book, little bird." I nodded toward the rumpled sheets she'd lain in before I arrived. She laughed while crawling over me to sit in her spot.

"You know birds eat spiders, right?" she teased and I instantly needed to kiss her for it. Nothing got my goat more than her engaging in wits with me. I loved her mind and easing her out of her bookworm shell brought me more joy than stress eating. She made life a little brighter.

"Enough chatting about devouring me unless you want a repeat of the last time you couldn't stop tasting me." I lifted the book out of her hand and skimmed the page she was on. Her whole body tensed beside me, and I smirked. She was thinking about the moment I had kissed her in the library, and she moaned so loud someone had to remind her we were in a quiet place. The blush on her face kept a smile on my lips for hours. She grabbed the book from my hands and wiggled into her bed farther. I reached down to pull the blanket up over her body, and I leaned my head against the wall. When she started reading silently, I prodded her to read aloud. The sound of her voice distracted me, and my thoughts desperately needed it.

"'Your spark for knowledge . . . his eyes seemed to glow and I wondered if his fangs were down as well. I stared at him and thought about his deal.'" She read aloud and the lull of her voice and the story about a vampire named Tatsou consumed my mind. There was no room to worry about matters I couldn't control at this moment. After an hour of reading, her voice drifted off. My woman was fast asleep.

I twisted to the side and with a deep breath, I blew out the candle on her nightstand. Part of me wished I had the power of wind to blow the others out from the bed, but I didn't. I eased off the mattress and took care of every tiny flame until darkness covered the room. A gentle breeze passed through the air as I stared at Dris. We hadn't progressed in our relationship to sleeping in the same bed, and I didn't want to push her. We had time, and I refused to break her acceptance of me by rushing. The patient hunter always captured his prey. I'd learned that mindset a long time ago. You have one hundred percent chance of getting what you want as long as you keep trying for it. You have zero percent if you give up. I would have Dris as my wife one day, and I'd fight like hell to show her I was the perfect male for her . . . to be worthy of such a pure light in my world. With quiet steps, I stopped at her bed and leaned down to kiss her forehead.

"Stay with me," she whispered, and I smiled. Her hand crept out of the blanket and wrapped around my arm. Those delicate fingers pulled me down. Not wanting to disappoint, I eased on top of the covers and kicked my boots off the side. She turned over and wrapped a leg and her other arm across my body. I was definitely winning our little game. Dris liked being chased, maybe because her intelligence frightened men off. I'd chase the owl Fae through every library on earth if she decided to go there. I fell asleep surprisingly quickly, and the nightmares showed for their scheduled programming.

29

Darkness everywhere. I couldn't even see my hand in front of me. I wasn't dead, although the pain in my back made me wish for death. As soon as the trap doors opened, I knew I was a goner. It wasn't going to be a monster or war that killed me, but a damn fall to my end. The scent of blood and rotten flesh made me gag. I wasn't sure I wanted to see what disgusting sights surrounded me in this space. My friends were looking for a way to find me while I'd search for my own exit. My poor beast Jengo didn't make it and the sound of his body hitting the rocky ground replayed in my head.

I shuffled my steps with a hand out to check for walls or obstructions. Twice my fingers met wet and cold bodies hanging from the ceiling of a cave. The smell of corpses and the feel of their blood was too much. I raced through the tunnels, tripping on bones, and fell into a pit that wiggled against my body. Sharp pains tore through every bit of exposed skin, and I reached blindly for a way out. The unmistakable feeling of scales on wiggling snakes pulled a string of curses from my lips. A hanging root was my salvation away from being eaten by hundreds of snakes underground. I was going to die down here, and I'd never get to see her face again.

Lips pressing my cheek woke me up, and my eyes sought the light coming from the opened window.

"Nightmares?" Dris's calm voice asked between sweet pecks against my skin. I breathed in deeply and remembered I did, in fact survive, that awful dwelling of the Vipereon back at Harold's Deep. I did get to see Dris's face again.

"Yeah," I admitted, and turned to give her more than my cheek to connect her lips with. We hadn't had sex, but I knew from the way this woman kissed that she was a librarian in the streets and feisty between the sheets. Worth the wait in every single way. Her tongue flicked my lip piercing, and all memories of that horrid place fled back into the depths of my mind where they belonged. Her hands wrapped around my neck, then weaved through my hair. Her delicate fingers grasped onto my horns and pulled me closer. Her need took over control of her body, and hell if I didn't enjoy it. I rolled over and took her body with me to settle on top. She chuckled and continued to strategize how best to consume me through her touch.

"Touch me, Emrys," she demanded, and my hands went straight for the robe she'd been grasping at last night. It was like unwrapping a present, and my greatest desire lay inside. Perfect soft gray skin and pale gray nipples greeted me from the see-through lingerie. My hands palmed them, and she moaned against my mouth. We kissed and touched for so long

I thought I'd combust. She wasn't ready to go any further than our heavy petting. I promised her over and over that she was worth waiting centuries for. She pulled back on our heated moment, and I held her in my arms until it was time for us to get up.

"I'm glad you stayed, Emrys." She hugged me at the door, and I kissed her head.

"Your room is my room," I joked and she shook her head.

"I don't think so, bud." She pushed me out of the room and I left with a huge-ass smile on my face.

Chapter Six

Sapphira

I'd made a friend in the desert, and named him Lucky. It took a while for the little creature to trust me, but he followed me around while I walked along the coast looking for another town. I gave him food whenever I could and just when I thought he'd disappeared, I heard him sleeping near my shelter with his little pig snores.

After a day of walking, I changed into a dragon, and Lucky ran away. I grabbed my bag of supplies and looked for him. Not wanting to leave the creature behind, I walked at a normal pace and heard little hooves following behind me. If dragons could smile, mine would have reached my ears. We walked together and I dug more purple roots and held them in my clawed hand. It took a couple tries but my friend grew comfortable to sit in my hand. I probably shouldn't have wasted so much time trying to befriend the animal. I needed to get home, but an unknown pull within connected me to this creature. I had to bring him along.

In the end, I spent two days training my new friend to fly with me as a dragon. Miles flew behind us as I searched for someone with more information than me. There wasn't much along the coast lines except another empty town with tattered fishing boats against the shore. My suspicions led me to believe the apocalypse had destroyed this place beyond repair. People had died or evacuated. Verin's poison of the Heart Tree did unimaginable damage and ruined so many lives.

After an hour of flight, the land curved to the east and the water turned a turquoise blue. White birds dodged me as I zoomed by them across the water. Miles of water surrounded me when my stomach ached and my vision became fuzzy. I shook my head and pushed my wings to move faster and faster to the other side of the sea. It was still a turquoise blue, and if I looked down I could see the bottom. Land had to be near. The ache shifted into a pain across my abdomen, and I feared for the baby. Panicked, I frantically searched for somewhere to land so I could shift back into my Fae form. Every flap felt like slow motion. Lucky squealed in my hand and I narrowed my blurry sight ahead. There had to be land close. I could make it.

My vision went dark and I roared. I wanted to cry. Flying blind wouldn't help me find a safe haven. The power to remain as a dragon poured out of me, and the reality hit me that I wasn't going to find safety in time. I should have stopped to rest before flying over the water. My friend and I were heading into the sea. I pushed the pain out of my mind long enough to scent the water and flew downward. My tailed touched a chilled wave just as the agony of shifting tore through my body. We tumbled into the water, and down, down I went, my poor friend lost in the depths with me. A roar barreled from my chest and the cold liquid flowed into my throat. I blew all the air in my lungs out and thrashed to reach the surface.

My body burned like fire while at the same time began freezing at the tips of my fingers and spread toward my chest. My legs kicked and I thrashed my hands to blindly reach air, but there was none. I was too deep and had nothing left. A tightness wrapped around my chest and I fought harder. I couldn't die; too many people needed me. The world needed me to survive, to keep the child inside my womb alive. All magic depended on me. I reached deep with every molecule of my being to my reserve of magic and became fire under water. The ground beneath me rose and pushed me toward the surface.

"You have to stop!" Someone's gurgled scream echoed in my head and I inhaled deeply.

"I'm going to get you to the boat. Turn off your flames!" a man's voice commanded. I tried to will myself to stop but my mind was too far gone. Sudden pain laced through my skull and everything shut down. My body grew weightless, and I felt like I was back in the sky as a dragon. Wind blew against my face, and I was finally free of pain.

Icy-blue eyes stared into me from across the meadow. Those perfect lips I knew so well tilted into a smirk and I sobbed. It was him. My mate. Beside him tiny little fingers gripped his pants and then a dark ebony-headed girl with curls and light brown skin peeked from behind him. Her gray eyes watched me, and her pink lips frowned. My mate reached down to hoist her into his arms. He whispered something in her ear, and she smiled.

"She's waking up!" a woman yelled, and I winced. A groan slipped past my lips, and I clung to whatever dream I'd been in. Rune and a little girl.

"Oh thank goodness, I worried I'd hit her too hard." A man with a familiar voice sighed, and I tried to open my eyes. Light burned as the darkness that had blinded me before had vanished. A blue sky and a cream-colored snout welcomed me back to consciousness.

"Lucky!" I squealed, and the snout wiggled. Slowly, I rose and saw my precious friend standing beside me. He was OK. Tears sprang to my eyes. I thought I had lost him while losing myself. I peered around the wooden boat I sat upon and noticed two eyes staring at me from about ten feet away. A short woman with tan skin and light blue hair stood beside a sturdy man with shimmering scales on the side of his face.

"We saw you crash and rescued you. About scared us half to death. You were a flailing dragon, then shifted into Fae inches away from the water." The woman placed a hand on her heart and chuckled.

"We've never seen a dragon before, especially one with a creature in its claws. It was a scene from my nightmares." The man shook his head but had a soft smile on his face.

"Thank you," I whispered. My throat ached with the words. Like a smack on the back of the head, I remembered the pain in my belly. The baby! I looked at my stomach, my fingers moving over the material of my worn armor for signs of blood.

"Oh, um, I didn't mean to invade your privacy but I'm a healer Fae. I used my gifts to check you over and noticed your pregnancy. The baby is fine in case that's what's got you in a tizzy." The woman took a step closer, with an understanding expression.

"The baby is OK?" I wanted to weep and I placed my hands over my stomach wishing I could check for myself. As if on cue, a little flutter tickled me, my baby letting me know she had survived, too.

"Yes, ma'am. Once we get back to the city, we can give you a proper checkup." The man nodded with his wife's words, then walked to the helm. His eyes focused behind me.

"What city?" I croaked and looked at the water to my left and then right.

"Regno Dei Lupi, the kingdom of wolves." The woman beamed with pride and I twisted around. Turquoise waters met with tan cliffs and tall buildings and a great white wall. The structures snaked up the cliffs inland to where a magnificent palace with white rooftops glistened like the night during a full moon.

"Wait, did you say Regno Dei Lupi?" The memory of that kingdom from across the sea popped into my brain. I'd forgotten where I knew it until just now.

"Yes dragon, this is our home."

It was Rune and Tor's home, too. Up that winding cliff, sitting in that stunning palace, was a cruel king they called Father.

Chapter Seven

Sapphira

I did my best to help Aminthe and her husband, Amund, dock the boat, although I'm sure they would have done a better job without me getting in the way. I scooped Lucky into my arms and followed behind them to their home. People cleaned fish off the side of the boardwalk, and a few of them had scales on the side of their faces, too. Bright blues, yellows, and greens shimmered in the afternoon sun. The outskirts of the city danced with life. People chatted with each other, cooking, and older couples sat outside their homes. My guides waved to all who hollered their names, and I gave the strangers a polite smile. I knew my faded armor drew attention to me, as did the creature in my arms, but no one said anything.

Their home was like the others, a townhome where everyone's outer walls were attached.

"All right, my dear, you may set your pet in the backyard and let's get you into my office." The kind woman gestured to the door beside her kitchen. Their yard was nice, they had wooden walls around the grassy and rocky area of the cliff for privacy. I set Lucky down, and he joyfully ran around before rolling in the grass. I closed my eyes and appreciated this moment of peace. The wind caressed my cheeks and scents of lemon and rosemary wrapped around me. I gagged. The scents overtook my nose, and I ran back inside.

"I couldn't stand to go outside while I was pregnant, either. My neighbor loves that scent and has about a dozen rosemary plants in her garden." She lifted her hand for me to take, then guided me through the homey living room containing blue furniture and wooden tables. Her office looked like the healer's quarters back home, and I sat on the padded table.

"Let's give you a look, shall we?" I laid back and she closed her eyes. Both her hands stayed about four inches over my body. I felt them warm as she moved over me slowly, as if getting a reading on my health.

"Nothing is broken, no injuries, and your organs are in good shape." She paused her assessment over my lower abdomen. Her lips lifted, and I hoped that meant all was well.

"The babe is perfectly fine. A very bright and powerful energy grows in your womb." She opened her eyes to look at me for confirmation that her words were true and I nodded. She giggled once before jumping back to her observations. After some time, she finished and reported that besides needing some nutritious meals, the babe and I were fine.

"I will make us a great meal, and you can tell us about you if you like. Or not. Whatever you are comfortable with." Aminthe was kind as well as blunt, but I knew she was curious about me.

"That sounds nice. I appreciate your help more than I can ever express. Thank you." I'd think of a way to make it up to them. I tried to help Aminthe with making pasta, but ended up creating such a mess that she nudged me off to the side where I listened as she talked about their life. She was the healer of the people, her husband a fisherman, and her older son was a soldier in the royal guard. Her youngest son lived two doors down with his new wife. She beamed whenever she talked about her children, and I smiled, thinking of my face in the future when I can do the same.

"Dearest, I have urgent news." Amund rushed into the house and clasped hands with his wife. His piercing eyes stared into mine.

"Guards are coming; they heard the gossip about the newcomer. We must delay our meal while this is sorted out."

"You're not in trouble, are you?" I stood from my seat, my power vibrating beneath my skin. They looked at each other once, then back to me.

"Outsiders aren't allowed in the city without a permit from the king. No one on this level of the kingdom are gossipers, but someone from another level of the cliff must have seen you and reported you for a reward."

"I will talk to the king and handle this."

The knock on the door did not surprise us. Amund let the guards in silver armor walk inside the house, and they demanded I come with them. Aminthe grabbed Lucky for me, and I held him while we walked out of the house.

"Do you want us to go with you?" she asked, and I shook my head. I would find them before I departed. The king and I would need to have some words, and they shouldn't be burdened to hear them.

"Is that a—"

"My pet," I interrupted the guard who kept looking at my little friend and me.

"Do you know what it is you carry? Where did you get it?" Curiosity drove his words. The main guard leading the way shushed him, and his back straightened immediately.

We walked up the cliffs, and I saw the levels of people Amund spoke of. They lived closest to the sea and with the commoners—the fishermen, farmers, and lesser Fae. Kingdoms were always ruled differently than each other, as was their customs, but I considered this way my least favorite. In Crysia, the commoners and nobles lived together in the kingdom. The only difference was the parties. I assumed it was because the rest of the town didn't care to put on a show like the nobles did, strutting like peacocks to showboat their power. My jaw slacked as I took in the magnificent gates made of pearl and silver before the palace. Four guards nodded at their comrades as we entered. Gleaming jewels in the shape of shells dotted the stone walls, with statues of beautiful men and women lining the large pearl doors.

This palace was like nothing I'd seen before. Everything from the curtains, to the trim around various paintings shimmered like it was dusted from moonlight. Tor and Rune had grown up here; this was their home. It was lavish and screamed royalty.

Crysia was beautiful in a different way, however. We built the palace with nature, working together to enhance the beauty already in existence, as if the structures grew from the ground itself. This beacon of the kingdom was created to brag about the richness of their treasures.

We walked into a grand hall and a handful of people stood in front of a dais.

"Pardon the introduction my king, we had a newcomer in the lower levels." The lead guard spoke and bowed as far as he could in the armor. The crowd parted and I looked at the stone thrones. A black-haired man with a matching beard and icy blue eyes stared at me.

My future father-in-law.

Chapter Eight
Sapphira

"Who are you, newcomer?" the king bellowed. Those familiar eyes narrowed on my face and my pet, then widened. His hand shook as he pointed a finger in my direction.

"Who let that thing inside my palace?"

Guards from all sides of me rushed to grab my pet, and I shielded myself with flames. With swift moves a soldier managed to knock Lucky out of my arms, and I roared. The stone beneath my feet cracked, and Lucky squealed while dodging grabby hands. Suddenly, the crystals on his back glowed so brightly, my eyes instinctively shut. A mixture of screams and ear-shattering groans of pain echoed around the lush room.

"Kill it!" the king snarled, and I'd had enough. I reached to the ground and willed it to shake. A little fuzzy body touched my hand, and I opened my eyes to see Lucky completely unharmed. I grabbed him and stood.

"I am Princess Sapphira of Crysia. You will lower your weapons and cease your attacks against what is mine or suffer the consequences." I watched the king's reaction shift from shock to rage.

"You do not command me, child. I am a king, and you are in my kingdom. If I want to slaughter the creature that melted my men, then I have every right to." He glanced at the mess of melted armor and men on the floor.

Lucky did that? I'd have to teach him manners to let him know melting people is not a good way to say hello.

"You came after him, and he defended himself. As future Queen of Crysia and mate of the true heir to this kingdom, I advise you to wisen up your tone." I was in a shit mood, and my biases toward what this cruel king did to my mate drove my actions. He scoffed. "So you did marry Prince Torin, after all. Been a long time since I'd seen that boy."

"I did not marry Prince Tor, but as soon as I return to Crysia, I will become the wife of Prince Rune, the firstborn of your Wolfstrom line." I smirked, and readied myself for the outburst that would surely follow. This king needed to practice his anger like Rune suggested I do, lest he make mistakes from the distracting emotion.

"That cursed monster is no son of mine. I assumed he died and was grateful to be rid of him. The fact you mated with him over Torin says much about you, Princess." He schooled his anger with a mirroring smirk to mine.

"That it does. Well, now that you know who I am, I request to stay in the palace for a few days before continuing my journey home." I'd moved on from poking the king in his tender spots. There would be time for that later. I needed to rest, change out of my torn fighting leather, and eat something. After that, I would do my part as Princess of Crysia and fight for my kingdom. The king may hate my mate, but he sent his sons over with the purpose of an alliance. A war swiftly moved toward my home and having a few allies in my pocket would be useful. The king eyed me suspiciously and stewed on my words.

"Landon, place the princess in the Turquoise Room. She needs her rest if that extra tiny heartbeat in the room has anything to say about it." His gaze dropped to my stomach, and I masked my face to be unreadable. The Wolfstroms were mostly made of jewels and wolf essences. Superior hearing came with the territory.

"Indeed."

"We shall meet for dinner and discuss the matters at hand. For now, get out of my sight."

I was officially dismissed. What an asshole. No doubt my power display and my pet kept him from attacking me where I stood. However, that leniency would only last so long. He'd ferret out everything he wanted to know and decide his course of action. I hoped for at least one fight between us, so I could repay the pain he had caused my mate. The guard, the one named Landon, approached me and held out an arm. I kept my mouth shut as we left the throne room and the stench of melted bodies. Apparently, the baby didn't mind *that* smell. The halls of the palace were ornate with shells and gold. Paintings of vines with blue fruit hung close to the sea-covered stucco like wall.

"Turquoise Room," Landon announced in front of a door, and I pushed it open.

"I guess I know why they named it that." I stepped inside the bluish-green room and breathed deeply.

"Will he try to kill me tonight?" I blatantly asked the guard, and he winced. Lucky scrambled in my arms, and I set him on the stone floors. He wasn't potty trained, so I would have to take him outside as much as possible or find a way for him to go inside and I clean it. I wish I could grow a patch of grass on the floor.

"No." Warmth tingled up my hands, and deep down I knew he wasn't lying. Tor's gift was truth; maybe that's what this was.

"Thank you." I nodded and stepped farther into the room to glance out the large square window. Landon closed the door behind me, and Lucky walked in a circle by the bed and plopped down. His little snores echoed around the room moments later. Poor baby. Using whatever source of his power had exhausted him. Just as I started to sit on the fluffy

47

blue bed, a knock on the door had me jumping to my feet. The door opened, and a young woman rushed in, her blond head bowed.

"Sorry to rush in, Princess, but I was told not to delay. My name is Janera, and I am your servant for your stay. I will help you bathe, find appropriate clothing, and assist in whatever needs you have." She bowed and looked at me with glowing-green eyes. I sighed and sat back down.

"You're not going to assassinate me if I let my guard down, are you?" I half teased, and she giggled before catching herself with wide eyes.

"I'm so—"

"It's fine. You have a lovely laugh. I think a bath would be nice, but I'll wash myself. If you could fetch something for me to wear, I'd appreciate it. I don't have money but you can put it on the family tab." I winked and she giggled again.

"Yes, Princess."

She made haste past a door to my left, and I heard the water rushing out of a faucet. Finally, I'd get to wash the desert and salty water off my skin. I knew I looked like a mess. When I faced the king later, I would need to look like the badass princess I was. Before I left for home, I would convince him to come to Crysia's aide.

"We're safe for now, little one," I whispered to the babe and a little flutter responded. We were gonna make this work. We'd be OK.

Chapter Nine

Rune

My queen had everything handled with a dragon by her side. I repeated those thoughts as I loaded up my mega-bear Silvio and left Crysia. It took only a day for me to conclude I couldn't wait for Sapphira to come home. I needed to do something. I'd collapse any kingdom who stood in my way. Since magic had returned, Fae and animals were more lively on the continent. Where before the land seemed desolate, now traveling groups and tradesmen scurried about. Possibly they'd feared for their life and safety before. With their essence at full power, their confidence to fight or run away gave them courage. I didn't talk to anyone and kept my hood up to cover my face in shadows. Still, I had the sense I was being followed.

I pushed Silvio up the rocky terrain toward Verin's territory. There would be no campfire, and only resting for short segments. No doubt he had scouts scattered around in search of soldiers or potential princess rescuers. Silvio's belly grumbled as night fell upon us, and I jumped off near a rocky ledge for protection over our heads. He ate one bag of red berries beside a stone I'd shaped into a bowl to hold water. The moon's light made the beast within growl to be released. When Sapphira was around, I was able to control my curse, switching from Fae to wolf instantly. Without her, the wolf didn't care if I needed to become Fae again, it only listened to his mate. A stick broke twenty feet away, and I kicked a head-size stone into the air and punched it in the direction of the sound.

"You nearly killed me," an idiotic voice called from the darkness, and I sat back on the ground.

"I should have known," I grumbled and dug through my bag for the food. Tor walked with his unicorn into view, and I handed him a small package of chicken and beans. I'd hunt something if we ran out of rations. He moaned and snatched the food hungrily. Mars trotted over to Silvio and drank from the water beside him.

"You're off on a mission, and you weren't hiding it that well. I'm in for finding Sapphira, and I got your back." He sat on a large rock and chomped on the food. I was quicker and stealthier without others to watch out for. Now I had to keep an eye on my little brother and the woods.

"I guess I better announce myself, too." I groaned and closed my eyes at the newcomer. Tor wasn't the only one following me. Emrys stepped out from behind a tree with Cara, Sapphira's recovered-from-battle catagaro.

"Anyone else joining me on this venture?" I growled, and the thunderous flapping overhead answered my question. A bright light flashed for a moment, then Desmire strode to our group.

"You all are supposed to be protecting Crysia." My soldiers could handle an attack, but knowing they were there to fight eased my mind.

"You're not searching for her alone. If you die, my daughter will never forgive me." Desmire sat and lit a fire for us. Then dared me with an arched eyebrow to challenge him. I growled, ready to fight the male when he spoke.

"I scanned the woods before shifting. There is no one around. Ease your beast, son." He smiled and graciously took the food Emrys snatched from my bag for himself and the dragon. Great. Fucking great.

"Now that the gang is all here, what is the plan?" The goat Fae broke the growing silence, and I sighed.

"Break into Verin's palace undetected, find Sapphira, and go home." Once I got a layout of the structure, I'd add more details. There was no intel on what his place looked like that I could plan accordingly.

"Good plan, but what if Sapphira isn't there?" Tor asked, and I stared at the bright moon with hope.

"Then I'll keep searching for her," I stated flatly, and everyone nodded. This group was all-or-nothing in this rescue mission. I hoped I'd made the right decision leaving Crysia, but my heart wouldn't allow me to sit by.

"Boys' trip!" Emrys hollered and shoved food into his mouth with a grin. My hands ran down my face, and I shook my head.

After eating, we took shifts sleeping, and Desmire claimed the first time slot to stay up. My body screamed for more than a few hours' rest, so I happily laid on the grass beneath the ledge to close my eyes. However, despite needing the sleep, I woke up when a fresh log collapsed on the fire.

"Worry not, son, we needed more tinder," Desmire whispered, and I glanced at the two sleeping bodies near me. Neither of them were up, and the sky was still dark. Sunrise was probably a few hours away, but I wasn't going back to sleep now.

"I'm not your son."

"Not yet. I assumed I need to get accustomed to the usage since you are planning to wed my daughter." He smirked, and his gray eyes swirled in a mysterious way. I shrugged, then moved closer to the fire. I would marry Sapphira, and technically he would be my father-in-law, the infamous dragon Fae and warrior.

We stayed silent until the morning, content to watch the woods and listen to nature's whispers, sounds only an animal could hear. The ground vibrated with life, the trees connected to every living thing on earth, and the wind sang to all who know the language. The dragon and I were not so different from each other. Big brutes whose legendary creatures'

53

sides were brought to heel by their strong-willed mates, dual cores bound by love. I liked that he didn't feel the need to constantly talk like the other two.

From the moment they woke, their chatter silenced the wind's song and Desmire shook his head. They were humorous to him and annoying to me. I cared for them, brothers of my kingdom, but if I could tape their mouths shut, I probably would.

"Verin's palace isn't too far, maybe a few days' ride. There is a wall with a constant fire across the top before his volcanic castle," Desmire commented, and I nodded.

"I've kept an eye on the place over the years, waiting to see my brother so I could scorch him." He shrugged before hopping onto Cara. Emrys was again riding with someone else like the last journey we went on.

Seeing a dragon in the sky near his home would alert Verin of our arrival. Discretion was our advantage. I'm sure between a werewolf, a dragon, an invisible goat Fae, and an expert archer, we could figure out how to get past the wall and rescue the princess.

Chapter Ten

Dris

"I can't believe those assholes!" Nyx stomped into the library and I covered my ears.

"They just left to go on a mission without us!" She made it to where I sat at the table with two books in front of me, then paced. It had been a few days since the boys left for a rescue mission, and Nyx still fumed. They all left a note in some way except Desmire. He told his queen he was off to help find their daughter. I glanced at the bouquet of flowers Emrys left as his note. There were various flowers mixed in, but I worked his puzzle out in no time. Azaleas meant take care of yourself for me. The sweet pea represented a goodbye, and the red camellia spoke of his longing for me. They'd come back. Rune had disappeared first and I thought it was odd, but it wasn't long before the others were gone, too. They would help find our princess and bring her home.

"They will be back." I grabbed the book and brought them to their organized place on the shelf.

"I know they will come back. I mean, I hope they don't get hurt in the process." She sagged into a chair, and I floated over to her.

"They will come back and until then, we are helping to hold down the kingdom." I hugged her, and her fingers gripped me tightly. I knew she worried about Tor. Their relationship had been growing intensely since we arrived back in Crysia. I wouldn't be surprised if they decided to marry soon. They bickered back and forth, but then they would look into each other's eyes and find peace.

"Right. You're right. I just miss him, which seems silly to say since our relationship is so new." She sighed, and I released her only to look into her purple eyes.

"You are mates. That connection is eon's old, and when separated, you feel like you're missing a part of yourself. Everything that I've read about mates and seen in others is that the bond inside you is searching for its match every second. The farther away you are from each other, the greater the ache in your chest."

Tears brimmed on the edge of her eyes, and she nodded. Having a mate sounded both exhausting and exhilarating at the same time.

"Thanks, Dris. I think because it's so new, and these feelings are so strong that it's making me a little crazy. What if Tor changes his mind about me? We didn't like each other for so long, and now, he's been so patient and caring. Honestly, he's everything I ever wanted in a guy," she rambled, and I pulled her back into my arms.

"We owl Fae see all remember, and Tor is nuts about you. When you're together, you look very at ease, and he watches you even when you don't see it."

"I know. Tor does really like me. I know it's not just the mating bond, it's more than that. I really like him, too." She laughed and pulled back.

"Never would have seen this coming, but it oddly works. He complements me in many ways. I need to keep the faith." She fanned her eyes to help compose her emotions.

"So what is on the agenda for today? Enough about me. I need a distraction." She patted her hands on the table, ready for me to take her mind off things.

"I don't really have much to do, unfortunately. The queen is very busy. The armies are making sure everyone is safe. Even the town has been put on high alert. Go about life as normal but be ready to hunker down when needed. You can head with me to the oak shelter. I'm supposed to help come up with ideas for safety. Should war arise, the people can remain safe inside it. However, with Verin being our king for some time, we have to double-check he didn't ruin anything." I grumbled the last part. Verin could have done anything from creating a back tunnel or breaking the locks. Nyx's chair scraped across the stone floors as she stood.

"That sounds good. I can help with some extra protection." She grinned and I nodded. Amethyst was great for protection; she could sprinkle some along the perimeter. We walked past the cave where my aunt Celestine used to reside, and I thought of her presence. She hadn't been in there for some time, which worried me. Her wisdom always came right when you needed it. If only I had more to offer like she did. The hundred-foot-tall doors made of solid wood greeted us at the entrance of the shelter. Pride blossomed in my chest at the sight of the giant symbol of Crysia in the thick grain. Three guards waited for us, and then we entered together.

"Nothing feels off; no weird vibes so far," Nyx commented, but I kept my keen sight on potential traps. The stone cavern went on for a mile and was at least five-hundred-feet tall. The queen had reinforced the walls with diamond to prevent collapses during war. It was impenetrable from the outside.

"Just keep looking and watch out for traps. Verin had many years to sabotage it." As Nyx and I walked along the edge, she cleansed the area with her powers while sprinkling amethyst on the rocks. I hadn't found anything dangerous yet, but I kept looking.

"We should stock the shelter ahead of time with blankets, food, and water. Everything we can for when Verin comes." I hated to say when he came, but it was a fact. Verin would come for Crysia. He needed to take out our queen, her mate, and their daughter. If he succeeded, then the rest of the world would easily fall. I shuddered and briefly closed my eyes. I couldn't think that way. We would fight, and we would win.

"All right I don't see anything. We should make a list of the supplies we have and—"

A tiny clicking noise was followed by the sounds of shattering glass.

"Everybody head for the exit," a guard shouted, and Nyx pushed me toward the door. I smelled it before I saw the white fumes. We were only ten feet away from the exit when the coughing started, then came spots in our vision.

"I think I'm gonna—"

Nyx fell to the ground and vomited. Crap, this wasn't good. My stomach churned and I knew I was about to join Nyx and the guards.

"Help!" I called out to anyone nearby, hoping they found us an antidote soon. I vomited onto the grass and saw people leaving their homes to run to us through my blurred vision. My body gave out, and my fingers grew cold.

"Help," I whispered and lost consciousness.

I vaguely heard a stone-scraping noise and people talking. My lungs craved a deep breath, and I tried hard to inhale only to gasp loudly. Footsteps ran to me, and I felt a hand on my shoulder.

"Myandris, you need to rest. I was able to remove the poison from you and your friends, but you need to rest." The healer Rista's voice attempted to soothe me, and I relaxed. I guess she had to use my full name to exaggerate the importance of resting. I tried to open my eyes but a sweet smell relaxed every muscle, and I fell back into the peaceful darkness.

Chapter Eleven

Sapphira

"I can't believe you said that! The king's face turned cherry red." Janera, the handmaiden, laughed with a sip of her tea.

The sweet female had become a friend during my stay these past few days as my powers regenerated. She helped me get ready for my meetings with King Natharrin Wolfstrom and provided many fun conversations. He attempted many times to ferret out my secrets and determine why I was in his kingdom. But I had no secrets. I told him of the war, of Verin, of his sons, and he still thought me to be keeping something from him.

"Rune is a better man than him and stronger. I told him he could accept my offer to be allies, to help in this war, and I would give it my best to convince Rune not to take his rightful place on the throne." I shrugged and sipped my own tea.

The baby wiggled and I placed my hand over my growing bump. It wasn't large but it wouldn't be too long before I'd really show. Aminthe and her husband were able to come visit, and she checked on the little one when she could. I knew I'd depart soon, but not without leaving the king with words to think about. Lucky squealed twice beside me. My hand drifted over his head to soothe whatever dreams made him speak. I missed home. Spending time in new places was great, but there was no place like your own bed with those you love.

"We thought those creatures were hunted to extinction. The crystals on their back harness the rays of the sun. They are able to unleash that power at will. Scary yet cute. Anyway, I bet I would love it in Crysia. It sounds so amazing by the way you describe it." Janera wistfully looked out the window to the waves crashing against the cliffs.

"You should visit sometime. I'll show you around." I nudged her and closed my eyes briefly. Having someone to talk to calmed me. Being alone in the desert made me realize how much I needed social contact.

"You're so different than any princess I've met. None of them would allow a servant to sit and drink tea by their side, let alone be so casual with conversation."

I opened my eyes and smiled at her. "I'll take that as a compliment. I've never been one of those princesses. I much prefer being with my people and nature."

A knock on the door interrupted us and Janera stood instantly, setting her tea down. She rushed to grip the handle, then opened it with wide eyes.

"Your majesty." The maid bowed low and stepped out of the way. A beautiful woman with brown hair and brown eyes walked in the door. A crescent shape crown sat in her wavy curls.

"Leave us," the woman calmly demanded but her tone left no room for argument. Her rich brown eyes roamed over the room, then over me. Her unreadable expression masked whatever conclusion she found after her assessment of me.

"You are pregnant with my grandchild?" She strode to my sitting area and slowly sat in the chair. I poured her a cup of tea, to which she stared at briefly.

"Yes, Queen." She must be Rune and Tor's mother. She didn't smile . . . only watched me with a familiar stare. Rune had his father's looks, but he inherited his mother's icy demeanor. Her blue dress matched the room but the golden embroidery shimmered in the sunlight. Luxury and elegance oozed from her pores as she handled the teacup and drank.

"I'm not a monster, you know. I kept Rune's other core from his father as long as I could. When I learned about the cruel things he'd done to my boy, it was too late."

This unexpected conversation surprised me. I'd yelled at her husband about his cruelty toward my mate, forcing Tor to marry a stranger. She hadn't been in the room during either meeting.

"Rune was always so strong, such a fighter. Even as I labored with him for many moons, I knew he was destined for greatness. Natharrin almost squished the light in his heart. Although I will admit part of me is grateful for the path destiny guided him to. Had my husband liked him, Rune would have become his mirrored image.

"Tor was a gift to our broken family. My husband had strayed with a human in the other realm. She gave him to us, and I loved him as my own. I'd hoped he would give Rune a sense of family that he hadn't felt before." Her eyes glistened and I wanted to touch her hand, but I didn't know if she'd deem it inappropriate, especially given my powers of absorption through touch.

"Rune is very happy in Crysia. He's the general of our armies, many people respect him, and his men will follow him into any battle." Warmth grew within me and the baby responded to the happy sensations running through my body.

"I always wanted a grandchild to spoil." The right corner of her pink lips lifted.

"Help me save my home, your sons, and this baby. It's going to take all of us to beat Verin," I pleaded.

She set her tea down to place her other hand on top of mine. "I wanted to meet you, see what type of woman you are. Rune has the gift of earth and his werewolf. Tor holds the gift of truth. My youngest son is a lot like me in many ways, choosing duty over heart, stability over freedom. Within seconds I saw your heart, and I am grateful my son has a strong and spirited mate. You will be wonderful parents." She nodded and gently set her hands in her lap before standing.

"Thank you for the tea." She bowed her head, then moved to the door.

"Will you help us?" I pleaded once more and she stopped, hand gripping the handle. Her head tilted to the side, and she smiled. She said nothing as the door opened and she left me staring at the air where she'd stood.

What did that smile mean? I groaned and wanted to fight something. I was grateful for the chat with the queen. She seemed nice, and I'm sure we could chat for hours but my time was running out here. I needed an answer. After moments of brewing in my thoughts, I called for Janera and she helped me into a beautiful black dress and I fashioned a sapphire crown on my head.

Chapter Twelve

Sapphira

The queen sat beside the king as I kicked the door open with a gust of fire. I was here to make a statement. Lucky squealed beside me, his little hooves stomping louder than usual. He meant business, too.

"What is this?" the king growled, and three guards stepped closer to his throne for protection. I stomped the ground and a fissure tore into the earth from my heel to their feet. The guards jumped out of the way and the king's eyes widened. He feared his son's power, but I held that greatness inside me and more.

"I am leaving in the morning to go home, and I demand an answer. I'm tired of your royal games. Will you ally with Crysia to help save the world from Verin's evil grasp? Will you help your sons, the future rulers of your kingdom?" The ground rumbled as my impatience grew. Fire leaked from my fingers, and I breathed deeply to calm myself. Losing control more than I already had could damage this very flimsy truce we had. Instead of being let go peacefully, I may have to fight my way out. The queen leaned down to her husband's ear and whispered. Despite my excellent hearing, I couldn't tune into the words flowing from her pink lips. His expression hardened as she smirked against him.

"I do not take being commanded to lightly, Princess of Crysia. I could end your life for such impertinence," he stated, and I waited for some further insult to be slung my way with a sign. However, as the minutes dragged on, he continued to stare at me with calculating eyes.

"Better get used to being commanded if Verin takes over Crysia. You think he will stop there? He will cross the oceans. He will portal-jump his army and destroy everything. This beautiful kingdom and your people will fall to an infinite age of darkness. You don't have to like me, and I may never forgive you for what you did to my mate, but we can still come together to fight the bigger enemy." I stood tall and let all the absorbed essences within give me the strength I needed to face their answer.

"You're right, Princess. I do not like you. I believe you to be feral and childish flashing your powers around like you are some goddess. You are arrogant and that smart mouth of yours will get you punished. I think you're a fool for mating with that savage beast instead of Torin. Nonetheless, I can ignore those faulty traits in order to keep my kingdom. I will send what armed forces to Crysia that I can spare. But listen here, girl. After this battle, you and that cursed wolf will not step foot on my shores again. Prince Torin will come back and prepare for his birthright to accept the crown with your full support as an ally. Do we agree?"

It was the king's turn to wait while I digested his words. I hated making choices for others. If Tor wanted to come back then I'd support him, but I didn't want to ship him off kicking at my boots. Nyx being his mate would want to leave, too. I'd never heard Rune talk about returning to his homeland. I think he would gladly take this deal. The queen's brown eyes narrowed at her husband and the hint of a sneer snuck onto her face. Her disdain for the king's deal spoke volumes of her true feelings. She meant everything she had said earlier.

"I vow that Rune and I will only return if our assistance is needed. As for Tor, he will come when he is ready to. He is not a member of my kingdom to delegate. You may have words with your son when you see him before battle." It was the best I could do. Whenever Tor became king, he could change these rules and or request our assistance for anything, including silly things like helping him drink a bottle of wine.

"Once the battle is over, he will come home."

"That's for you and him to discuss." I stood my ground. He needed this alliance and he knew it. Verin would destroy everything. As a leader, he understood the more people that faced the tyrant, the better our chances were.

"Fine. Now get out of my sight. I don't want to see your face until we meet at Crysia in three weeks." He shooed me away with his ring-covered fingers and I smiled. The queen nodded after giving me a wink, and I took my leave. I thought about staying and going back to Crysia with the army but I couldn't wait. I'd secured a map thanks to Janera's help, and now I had a course home. I could borrow a boat to sail across the great ocean but that was a perilous solo journey. The best route was for me to head northeast. There were a few kingdoms I could ask to help before flying over the two-point-four-mile straight and then I'd only be a two-day flight away from home.

I strutted through the palace and changed into a pair of wide-legged pants that tied at the top and again at the ankles with a comfy long-sleeve blue shirt that protected me from the afternoon sun while keeping me cool. I'd leave early tomorrow, so I walked to the lower levels to see Aminthe and Amund. They'd been so kind, and I wanted to see them before my departure.

"I wondered if we would be seeing you before you left." Aminthe answered the door after my first knock. She welcomed me into her home, and I hugged her.

"I'm leaving tomorrow. If welcomed, I wish to plead my case for allyship with the twin leaders of Asil Tas. Then hopefully the Queen of Lunnaya Skala. If all goes well, I should be home by this time next week."

After one last squeeze, I walked to the chair at her kitchen table and sat down.

"Make sure you've packed enough food and water. This phase of the pregnancy is vital for nutrients." She pointed a finger at me before resuming her vegetable chopping I'd completely interrupted.

"Yes, I know. I've got a big bag packed. I should be able to carry Lucky and it across the lands with ease. Shifting takes a lot out of me, so I will pack extra food."

"Oh, yes! I almost forgot. I need to show you how to use my gifts of looking into the body. It may come in handy during the upcoming war." She threw the chopped onions and carrots into a soup. I hadn't told her about my power of absorption, since it's not something I tell many people.

"When reading the body, it spills all the tea, so to speak. I know of your power and I'm honored to have given you a piece of myself. May it help you when you need it most." She grasped my hands, then dragged me to her office space to teach me how to assess a person's health with my hands.

Chapter Thirteen

Emrys

We made it to the outskirts of Verin's territory, and my life had been threated twice already. Good times with the boys. We hunted, and Tor and I chatted while the grumps sat by the fire in silence . . . my best friends in the realm. I mean, if someone doesn't want to murder you at least once, are they even your friend?

"I found some burberry beans," I announced, walking back to the camp. Rune fashioned us a cave of sorts for cover and camouflage.

"Nice," Tor commented and the other two grunted.

"I'd washed them in the stream so no worries about getting sick before the big rescue mission." I unloaded the little blue beans out of my untucked, folded-over shirt onto a plate. Our plan required lots of food and lots of sleep. I would sneak around as my invisible self to find a way in without being noticed. I offered to do the whole mission on my own since this type of thing was my specialty, but they denied it. If I got in a bind, I would be out of luck. Safety in numbers and various powers was the reason we all joined

Rune. We wanted to help find the princess and make sure the general stayed alive.

"I hope the girls aren't pissed at us," Tor said, his head tipped up to the stars. "We left so abruptly, I wouldn't blame them if so."

"Mine isn't." Desmire smirked and poked the fish hanging over the fire. The queen could handle everything while he was away and wanted her daughter back.

Dris would decipher my flower message and understand. She was my smart girlfriend. She'd keep working to make sure Crysia was ready for war with every sentence she'd ever read. Nyx, on the other hand, was a newly mated woman. Emotions tended to be irregular. Tor smiled often, made jokes, and acted himself for the most of our short trip. There were times, though, when he couldn't hold the smile and longing took over his expression. He'd rub his chest to soothe the ache, but only his mate had that power.

"Sapphira is pregnant," Rune grumbled while looking at the moon, as he did often. Desmire smiled then slapped the werewolf on the back, and Tor choked on a burberry bean.

"I'm gonna be an uncle," he gasped through his coughing, and leaned over to give his brother a hug. I wanted to join the hugfest but I let the brothers have this moment. Their kinship had grown into something of awe over our last journey . . . from hating each other to acting like family.

"Happy for you, General. I can't wait to babysit!" Thoughts of all the mischief the child and I could get into crossed my mind. Playing tricks on the parents and hide and seek in the library to ruffle Dris's feathers. Oh, the things we would do.

"So she was pregnant during the battle with the Dramens and Lethirya?" Tor winced and Rune nodded.

"She will not be sidelined because of our child. I'd like to see you try to make her sit in the palace and watch." Rune chuckled and Tor agreed. The princess would not take kindly to being shoved away to play pregnant princess while others fought. Good thing her skin could turn hard as a diamond like her mom's.

"A second chance to spoil a child as it grows." Desmire's normally hard face softened, and I knew he would instantly be wrapped around that child's finger. He unhooked the cooked fish and we all dug into our own.

"Did you get to see Sapphira as a child?" I asked curiously. Despite the jokes about our boys' bonding trip, letting things out before battle was essential. It eased the tension in the body and cleared the mind of lingering emotions. The dragon looked at me, and I stilled my body not to flinch from his piercing gray stare.

"Not very often. Sapphira's safety relied on Verin thinking he sired her. If he knew she was mine, he'd have killed her without remorse. I was there when Olyndria birthed her. She labored so hard, it broke me to see her in so much pain. Then my little girl entered the world. Brown curls and green eyes stared at me before her little cries echoed around the room. Verin had left his wife at the end of her pregnancy for hunting. I appreciated that he wasn't the best husband. It gave me time I would never had gotten otherwise."

The fire crackled . . . the only sound in the forest. Everything, even our breaths, stilled. I don't know how he did it. To watch your mate be with another and let that evil man raise his daughter while watching from the forest. I'm not sure I had the inner strength for it. Rune and Tor glanced at each other briefly. Perhaps they recognized this situation could have happened to them if Sapphira had married Tor before the apocalypse. Everything worked out in the end, and that's what we needed to remember.

"I bet Sapphira's growing a girl. You'll get your chance again. Maybe she'll even have her granddaddy's gray eyes," I offered, and the dragon thanked me for my words. Then the distinct sense of someone watching me crawled over my skin. My head lifted to find Rune nodding once, a precious gift of approval from the stoic Fae.

"Oh man, you are so in trouble if it's a girl. Then you'll have two feisty females to deal with." Tor laughed and his brother grinned so big I thought his face would break.

"A werewolf and dragon mixed in one body. A powerful and deadly combination," Desmire added and slid Rune a mischievous look. Poor general, he would have his hands full. But I knew he'd enjoy every second of it.

"What about you, Spider? Think Dris will make an honest man out of you?" Tor asked, and I feigned a dreamy sigh.

"I expect a proposal as soon as we get back. She's hopelessly in love with me," I teased, but in reality Dris was in love with me and I knew it. I could feel it when she looked at me. I just needed to show her it was safe to love me . . . that I wouldn't hurt her.

"You are hopeless." Tor chuckled with a mouthful of fish, very unprincely. He added, "I'm happy that you guys are together. I'm rooting for you."

"Same with you and Nyx." I winked and the prince blushed. The energy of our camp changed dramatically from when I had come back with the beans. Every male had love and hope for the future as a driving force. With that passion, we would not fail tomorrow.

Chapter Fourteen

Rune

Emrys thankfully didn't need to remove his clothes as he turned invisible to sneak into the castle. I'd created a gap in the wall for him to slide through from the tree line, then closed it behind him. We waited in silence, watching the giant wall with fire blazing on top. After some time, I felt the soft vibrations of the Spider's footsteps and opened another gap with a stomp of my foot.

"There are two entrances and both are guarded heavily. We could fight our way in but we'd be fighting every step while looking for Sapphira. I suggest we use the plumbing. There are two culverts, one with water going in and the other pushing water out. Once in, Rune could open up the floor since they are made of stone and 'ta da,' we are inside." Emrys appeared beside me, using his hands to describe his findings from behind the wall.

"Any talks of Sapphira?" My heart squeezed in hopes that she was indeed here and this wasn't a fool's mission.

"Nothing. It's oddly quiet in there. Almost like they will be punished if they speak when not spoken to." The goat Fae's nose scrunched up like the thought of too much silence was abhorrent.

"What's the game plan, General?" Tor asked and the others looked to me, even the oldest of the group. Desmire's expertise overwhelmed mine by centuries. I ran over the details and sorted through the strategies of each. I wanted to get to Sapphira in a hurry but impatience rarely helped the situation.

"Emrys suggests we go in through the plumbing, so that's what we'll do." A true leader knew when to listen to others' strengths. The goat Fae was a spy; therefore, we would listen to him. The male grinned that I agreed. We spent five minutes devising a more intricate plan.

"It works if you're touching me, and I allow it. You've got to feel completely free. Once your control-freak tendencies get in the way, you won't be invisible anymore." Emrys warned us about his power, then held out his hands for Tor and me to take. Desmire smirked and I knew he found enjoyment in watching me squirm at holding hands with them. The dragon would wait until either Tor or I signaled him to shift for distraction purposes. He'd do his best to divert their attentions while we searched for my mate.

"Go on, son, hold his hand," the asshole teased and I wondered if Sapphira would be mad if I punched her dad. Just once. Tor lifted their joined hands and then he disappeared. I groaned and reached for Emrys's wiggling fingers. The male winked at Desmire before turning invisible. I looked down and saw my body but none of the others.

"You're still visible," my soon-to-be father-in-law announced, and I willed myself to be sightless.

"You have to feel free in order for it to work. Do you feel free right now?" Emrys asked. His hand gripped mine, then lifted it up and back down again.

"I'm not trapped in a prison cell. I'd call that free," I grumbled, and waited for something to change. It didn't.

"You have to give up control of your thoughts for now. Focus on something that makes you feel high, like you can do anything." He offered more advice and I tried.

"Think of that feeling of battle, running through the crowd, slicing as you go. Using your powers to rattle the earth," Tor chimed in to give me something to visualize, but none of it worked. There were very few instances where I felt true freedom. I'd grown having very little of it, and even the twenty years Sapphira was gone I felt tied to the day we'd reunite.

"I'll just find another way in." I let go of Emrys, tired of reaching for a feeling I didn't truly know.

"No. You will get caught. This is gonna work. You are the future king of Crysia, and your kingdom and woman need you." A hand gripped mine tightly, and I tried to shrug it off, then gave up.

"Freedom." I sighed and closed my eyes. I felt like an idiot, but he was right. I needed to make this work, and I trusted his opinion that this was the only way. I delved into my essence, my core, and reached for the sensation. I breathed deep and exhaled loudly through my nose. Giving up control was not something I did willingly. Freedom was being able to do what you wanted without resistance or restraint. When I'm in the werewolf form, I am free to my savage side. My body tingled, but I didn't stop thinking. Sapphira's face filtered into my thoughts. Her smile. Her damn mischievous and smart-ass mouth drove me into madness half the time. Memories of being with her in Crystoria, free to spend time with each other without the stares and the fear. My chest warmed. With her I could be myself, my true self, asshole parts and all. With her I was free to be who I was and not what everyone thought of me. I wasn't the cursed prince. I was just Rune.

"See." Emrys's voice brought me back to reality and when I opened my eyes, I saw their faces watching me. Desmire nodded and I looked down my body. I could see myself and a faint rippling of air around me. Interesting.

"Freedom is a good look on you, brother." Tor grinned and I nodded.

"Let's go." We awkwardly walked hand in hand to the wall. I stomped once and a gap to walk through opened up. After we cleared the wall, I slammed it shut. The castle looked evil, created on the side of the volcano with large metal spikes and black stone mix with obsidian walls. Red flags and a black fist with fire at its center moved alongside the light breeze from posts around the premises. A moat filled with black tar bubbled in front of his castle. Of course he would have a black moat. The charcoal-colored edges resembled hardened lava, which gave me a layout of the directional flow if the volcano erupted. I'd never worked with lava before but a curious thought drifted in my head. Could I manipulate it since it was molten rock? A small river curved at the backside of the castle by the two culverts. Clean water was sucked into one side, then gushed out into a powerful waterfall from the other.

"His kingdom looks awful," Tor commented.

The landscape revealed dark homes behind his palace without life and trees. It was worse than living in the desert. The barren lands were littered with random vents to which children jumped around while trying not to get burned. Soldiers monitored the hard streets, and the people cowered at their approach. The homes were made from anything they could grab and stuck together with the ingenious rock. Verin's people lived in destitution and fear. Monsters roamed, like they were the elite beings of the land. A horned gorilla-like creature with four arms swiped at a family of Fae, then climbed on the roof of their house to jump over and over. Anger bubbled beneath my skin, and I craved the destruction of this forsaken place.

"Let's find Sapphira and get out of here. We can save them by defeating Verin," Tor reminded me while his hardened face memorized every detail we saw. This world needed more healing than we knew. Getting rid of Verin would only be the start. We'd have to find a way to mend the damage within the hearts of the realms. As we neared the culverts, our joined hands weren't necessary anymore. We climbed through the heavy current, and I felt the vibrations of every step until an opening appeared.

Chapter Fifteen

Rune

We climbed onto the stone floor of Verin's castle with weapons drawn. The halls were bare, with torches lit every ten feet. I closed my eyes and listened for the heartbeats around us. There were maybe twenty. Odd. Two thunderous beats echoed in my ears, but I focused in on a tiny little flutter to hit my senses.

"Follow me." With silent yet steady steps, we moved through the halls, then became invisible against the walls when a soldier walked by. A knot formed in my stomach as I recognized the emptiness of the castle. A few hundred soldiers stood outside in the kingdom. We could easily slay everyone we came in contact with and make it out alive. A red creature who looked like a rhinoceros in soldier's armor stomped by, his big, black eyes narrowed in our direction. He continued onward. We turned a corner and up six stairs were two guards in front of a golden door. That had to be where they kept my mate hostage. The fluttering of a baby's heartbeat came from behind that barrier.

"Emrys," I whispered, and the spider knew what to do. He moved past me and seconds later, the two men grunted and fell to the ground. He reappeared with a set of keys and a smile.

"Dris taught me that move. You pinch certain points in the neck, and it knocks them out for a while. Such a smart bird." He chuckled, as his hand reached to unlock the door. Tor and I rushed after him as it opened.

"Sapphira?" I breathed into the room and scanned for my mate. The hope of finding her and our child crumbled at the sight of five Fae women, one with a pregnant belly.

"No more! I can't take it. I'll kill myself first." A blue-skinned woman lunged for me, and I held her wiggling body away before picking her up to deposit her back on the sofa she had come from.

"We're not here to hurt you. We're looking for Princess Sapphira. Is she here?" Tor stepped forward cautiously, and I growled a warning to the angry female not to lunge again. The pregnant woman stepped forward, her hand settling on her friend's shoulder. Her pale skin and golden hair shone like sunshine.

"Princess Sapphira is not here. The king's daughter left her in a sandy place across the great ocean. We know everything that happens with the king. This is his personal harem." Her melodic voice calmed the disappointment weighing me down. The failure of finding my mate stung. She wasn't even on this continent. I'd come here on a fool's mission.

"Harem? Like all of you . . ." Emrys asked, his face pinched up, and my thoughts mirrored the actions. The pregnant female nodded. The others were silent as they looked anywhere but our faces.

"We were all taken from our homes and kingdoms, brought here to service the king and his chosen men. He breeds us and takes our babes away to be hardened soldiers." She caressed her belly, and I shook my head. They were dressed in scandalous clothing, but a fierce fighting spirit glowed from each of their eyes.

"You're coming with us," I announced, and turned to the door. I would not leave these women to bear their fate. How could I look my mate and one day my child in the eyes if I deserted them? Sapphira may not be in this kingdom, but we can still do some rescuing.

"It's not safe . . . the guards." One of the quieter Fae spoke, her black eyes imploring us while her hair sparked purple, then blue.

"We can and will get you out of this kingdom," I vowed, and the leader of the woman nodded.

"There are minimal guards right now. The king led part of the army to Crysia, to test their forces." My heart hammered in my chest. We were here, and my kingdom was about to be attacked, if it hadn't been already.

"We're leaving now."

84

The women followed behind with only the wisps of clothes on their body as we led them through the castle. Tor silenced soldiers who saw our group with an arrow to the throat, and we kept moving. The blue female that tried to attack me led us through the maze of hallways to the exit closest to the moat and wall. A horn blared as we stepped into the sunlight and soldiers everywhere ran to us. Emrys knocked the guards in front off their feet and used the move taught by Dris.

"Out of the way, I have payback to deliver." The woman with the sparking hair pushed past me as I readied my power to take down the entire castle. Electricity sparked from her fingers, and the tips of her hair lifted toward the sky. Arrows shot at her but were blocked by streams of white-hot lightning shot from her fingers and spread across the ground. The discharge energy hopped from armor to armor as she released her gifts upon everyone in front of us. The woman wielded immense power. Once the men were dead or incapacitated, Tor asked the question we were thinking.

"If you had that power, why didn't you use it to escape when magic came back?" She blushed before answering him, and it was good to see the woman with confidence instead curling up with fear.

"Verin kept my powers sedated with one of his poisons. The last one I threw up before it spread into my system."

"Good job," I said, before the ground rumbled. I dug my foot into the stone walkway for stability before pushing up and leaping into the air. My fist hit the ground first as I landed. The earth rolled and rumbled as a shockwave tore into the wall and it cracked. Tiny splinters reached into every stone before wobbling unsteadily. Slowly it collapsed into a pile of ruin, the fire snuffed out beneath the rocks.

"We've got to go. Crysia is in trouble. I hear it on the wind." Desmire appeared through the dust, surprised by the women. His face hardened but then he shifted. The females gasped at the dragon. We walked to our beasts and lifted the women onto their saddles.

"Cara, Silvio, Mars. Take these women to safety, then come home." I directed the animals and each responded in a way that I knew they understood me. We'd be heading home on the back of a dragon.

"Thank you." The pregnant female smiled.

For now, the creatures would keep them safe and I knew they could protect each other with the one woman's power restored.

"To Crysia," I said, and the girls rode into the forest silently. Desmire roared. We jumped onto the dragon's back and he quickly took to the sky.

Chapter Sixteen

Dris

I missed the feel of the wind against my feathers. Flying felt like freedom after being trapped in my Fae form for so long. I could move silently through the sky and see everything perfectly despite moving so quickly. There were many advantages to being able to fly. I'd been soaring gently in the breeze when I saw movement on the edge of the mountains. Without being noticed, I'd kept to the canopy of the trees to scope out what caused such commotion of the land. An army marched for Crysia. Verin's soldiers and monsters that I'd never known existed swiftly moved to destroy my home. I rushed to the palace and warned Queen Olyndria. She reacted quickly, and the citizens were quickly evacuated to the cleared shelter. My flight had given us time to react.

"They've breached the southern border of the diamond wall!" Nyx yelled, and I shifted in the direction of the wall. Our queen had a wall made of diamond that rested deep in the earth, where it continued to harden over time. When war came to Crysia, she'd quickly raised the impenetrable barrier to surround her kingdom. No magic could break it, but that didn't mean enemies couldn't get over its points. I wiped the blood from my cheek, then lined up my arrow for the giant black lizard at the top of the wall. I may not have been born a warrior, but I'd grown to own the title . . . the librarian who not only used knowledge as a weapon but also a bow. I fired once, then quickly released another. It screamed as the sharp points embedded in the lizard's neck. The body fell to the ground with a loud splat.

"Nice." Nyx patted me on the back but my eyes narrowed on the red-and-black soldiers hopping over the fence. Our defenses had taken down about fifty soldiers who had entered the artisan's section of town. From what I could tell, there wasn't a strategy to this attack. It was a test, to see how prepared we were. Bet if I flew over the wall, I'd see a lackluster army. Yet, they weren't giving up.

"Let's go." I dug my boot into the dirt, then ran for the intruders with Nyx beside me. Soldiers of Crysia fell in step around us, swords and spears readied.

"Oak!" Najen yelled, and the female warrior to my right stopped to dig her fingers into the ground, and two oak trees burst forth beside the wall. Najen sliced every attacker on our side then jumped up the limbs as they grew. With one foot, he pressed off the trunk and launched his body over the wall. More of our soldiers joined him, and I debated if I should. I didn't want to get in their way. Rune had trained these men for situations like this, which involved protocols.

"Oh, I miss battle," a familiar voice bellowed and our queen in her diamond armor swung a dual-bladed staff. She spun it around like she was a performer, slicing into those who would hurt her with every step. Nyx and I stared, completely in shock that Queen Olyndria was so at peace on the battlefield. Sapphira definitely shared that family trait.

"I'm going to shift and see what's happening. Be safe." The breeze called to me, whispering to change now. Nyx nodded and leaped up the limbs of the new oaks, then hopped over the wall. I closed my eyes and in seconds my body whirled into a snowy owl. With a passing gust, I flapped high and saw the battle was indeed coming to an end. Twenty soldiers and three giant lizard men with elephant legs barreled their way into the fray only to be taken down by two of our Fae in bear form.

"To the north," the wind whispered and I tilted my body to turn. I noticed two figures at the edge of the Hallowstags Woods beyond the wall. Verin sat on the back of a monstrous, brown, three-headed snake with red scales peppering its belly. His daughter, Lethirya, lingered at his side on her giant red lizard she had at the Heart Tree. They watched with matching grins as their soldiers died attempting to take the city. My suspicions rang true. This was a test, a mere skirmish of the battle to come. Verin wouldn't waste his whole army with a blind attack like this. My heart stammered at the thought of his plans. I know we had injured men, probably some dead. This was only the beginning of things to come.

"North, north, north, north." The wind grew stronger, and I pushed harder in that direction. I was no match for Verin, and I knew fighting him was not my destiny. As I drew closer to the palace, I saw why I was called here. Our main forces were busy at the wall around our city. Few were left behind to guard the home of the queen. Two soldiers limped in front of the large wooden entrance with their swords ready. Ten of their companions littered the ground, their blood seeping into the soil.

This was not good. I screeched, alarming anyone who listened of the trouble at the palace. I wasn't sure I could take them all on and live, which was unfortunate. I had so many things I still wanted to do, like fully trust Emrys and let myself bask in his goodness. He was safe. I knew that. He only wanted me as I was. He loved my brain, he called me beautiful, he loved everything about me. I realized I loved the old goat. Now I really hoped I lived through this to tell him. My body shifted at the encroaching men, and I grabbed my bow as it popped back into existence. Arrow after arrow, I fired into the soldiers and the limping men sagged into each other.

"Smart girl. I like that in a woman."

A man wiped the sweat and grime from his face and threw a knife at my head. Jerk. I dodged it and leaped high onto his shoulders. Wide eyes stared at me as I chopped hard against his carotid three times. His body sagged instantly, and I flipped off him like I'd practiced the move hundreds of times. Soldiers in silver armor ran to us, and the remaining enemies scattered. We'd defended the kingdom and this test was over. I just wish I knew if we passed or failed. When the last man disappeared, I shifted again to search for Verin but he and his daughter were gone, his dead and injured soldiers left behind to rot on our lands. How very kingly of him. After two hours of scanning the kingdom for any hiding foe, and cleaning up the townsfolk's homes, the queen settled her warriors and walked back into her palace. We were safe for now.

"I don't know about you girls, but I could use a large glass of wine." The queen brushed past and waved us to follow her. I looked at Nyx and the maid who rushed to us with wet cloths to wipe the blood and dirt off.

"I could go for some wine. Might help me forget some of the things I saw today." She winced. We grabbed the cloths from the maid's hands and walked to the kitchen where the queen poured blue wine into three cups.

"What a day. As much as I love being in the midst of battle, I do not like losing any of my people. I fucking hate that coward, attacking us like that." She downed her glass in seconds, then poured another.

"Yeah." I couldn't say battle was my favorite pastime. Maybe getting drunk would help the sinking hardness in my gut lessen. I downed my glass. The sweet liquor coated my throat and warmed my body instantly. Nyx was already pouring herself another glass as I held mine out for more. Instantly, I swallowed it and then asked for more. The queen, Nyx, and I called for more wine and drank ourselves into a state of blissful escapism. Time passed and we laughed, and raised toasts to every thought that passed our muddled brains, until voices echoed throughout the halls.

"Nyx! Dris!"

"I think that's our names." Nyx giggled and passed the bottle to the queen, who laughed. Her finger reached in our direction as she whispered our names dramatically.

"Dris!" A dark-haired man with little horns and a lip piercing came into view and I smiled.

"My love! You made it!" I grabbed the bottle from Sapphira's mom and raised it in his direction.

"To you. You made it a little late to fight, but we girls helped defend the castle. You're the damsel in distress we aren't," I slurred and the handsome face I thought about burst into laughter. Beside him stood three men. The boys were back, and they had missed all the fun.

Chapter Seventeen

Emrys

"You asshole." Nyx glared at Tor and the male rushed to her side. Compelled to be with her, touch her, he reached a hand to caress her cheek and her anger melted.

"I'm ready to clean up and sleep, Emrys," Dris announced, and stood with her delicate hand outstretched for me. Instead of grasping it, I chose the safer route and scooped her into my arms. I looked at my friends. Desmire and the queen were already gone, and Nyx was cradled in Tor's arms. Time to get these battle-drunk ladies to bed. I hadn't noticed Rune slip out of the room, though I wondered if seeing this reunion with our women hurt. If Sapphira had made it home before us, she would have basked alongside her friends . . . without alcohol of course.

"I missed you," Dris purred as I carried her to her room, her head sweetly nuzzled against my neck. Without dropping her, I managed to open the door, then strode to her bathroom.

"Oh yes, I think I'd like to take a bath with you." She wiggled down my body and sprinkled some bath salts in the empty tub. I turned on the water and faced her bright eyes.

"Not tonight, little bird, but I will definitely take you up on a shared bath another time." I waggled my eyebrows, and she giggled in a very non-Dris way. How much did she drink? Even more reason for me not to get in the bath with her despite the desire to do so. I loved this girl, so I wouldn't be fucking it up in stupid ways like taking advantage of her intoxicated state.

"I thought about you earlier." She fiddled with the clasps of her torn coat and then the buttons of her high waist pants. I turned to give her privacy, even though I'd seen her nearly naked.

"Was I naked?" I teased, and I heard her clothes fall to the floor. My heart beat loudly, and my breaths stilled. Water sloshing in the tub told me she had submerged in the rising water.

"No, I was about to fight some of Verin's men and didn't know if I'd survive." She sighed, then silence grew in the room. She inhaled deeply, and I assumed she'd dipped her head under the water.

"Can you face me, Emrys?"

I shifted at her request and watched her survey my every move. Her normally wild and smoke-like hair lay flat against her chest, covering her breasts from my view. She looked every bit the magical creature she was, something out of a human's fairy-tale storybook.

"I'm not one hundred percent myself, but I think that helps me with what I'm about to do. I've been duped by guys who I thought liked all of me, but they didn't. Truthfully, you've always seemed dangerous to me. Not a sure thing or reliable. I judged you, and I'm sorry. You're pretty perfect for me. You think I'm pretty and smart and I like our banter." She swished her hands around the water, then turned the knob off with her toes.

"What I'm trying to say is . . ." She looked everywhere but me. "Octopuses lay 56,000 eggs at a time," she blurted, then dunked her head under the water. I withheld my laughter, knowing it would make this harder on her and I wanted to hear whatever thought that made her so uncomfortable. Once she resurfaced with droplets still falling from her lashes, she let it out.

"I love you. I'm nervous to say that, and scared, but it's also exciting. I don't know if I can give you whatever you're used to as far as women. I'm not sure I'm ready for sex but I—"

I pressed a finger to her moving lips. The front of my shirt grew warm and wet from leaning across the water to reach her.

"There is no one but you. Whatever we do is perfect. Your needs are not secondary to mine, and I love you as you are, with or without sex. We are partners, Dris. I'm not here to live for you, and you are not here to live for me. We live as ourselves and bring

95

that wholeness to the relationship." I hoped she heard my words in her muddled thoughts.

We joked with each other the majority of the time, or bantered, as she stated. But the realness of us was very serious. She nodded and changed subjects. Since she hadn't rambled a strange fact gave me hope that my declaration sat comfortably in her mind. I peeled my body back to the side of the bath and handed her a lavender-scented bar of soap from a basket beside me. She cleaned herself and I kept my eyes on hers or her light-blue decorated bathroom. Just because I was fine with waiting forever to have her didn't mean I needed to torture myself as her hands slid over her delicate skin. We filled the time with my tales of the boys' trip, until she yawned and I helped her dry, then dress for bed.

"It's your turn to read to me."

She tossed a book at me before climbing into her bed. She scooched over, leaving me enough room to get comfortable. I chuckled and plopped down in the given spot. This woman drove me crazy and kept me sane at the same time. She peered at me and intertwined her one hand with mine. Her eyes closed, and I rested the book against my legs and read aloud like she'd done with me. Barely a chapter into the story, little snores drifted through the air and I looked at my Dris. Today had been a busy day. Busy for sure, but a day I would never forget.

I stayed for hours next to my little owl Fae to bask in her presence. However, my gut instinct that never steered me wrong whispered I was needed somewhere else. Dris slept peacefully, and I'd come back before she woke. Slowly, I eased off the bed and smiled as she rolled over and hugged a pillow tightly. The halls were quiet as I followed my gut down the stairs, through the throne room, and out to the gardens.

The general sat on a bench, gazing at the nearly full moon. He heard my steps before I announced myself but didn't shift his attention to me.

"We're gonna find her," I promised, completely aware that my naturally joking nature wasn't fundamental right now. The man ached for his mate and the babe in her womb. I couldn't imagine being separated like they had for the majority of their relationship. They'd spent more time apart than together.

"I know. I feel her, if I quiet my mind enough, I can hear her. Sapphira always had a way with my curse, helping me transform to man during the full moon and calming the beast. She is my true moon. The ebb and flow of my world is tied to her." He smiled sadly. "I'm sure I sound like a lunatic."

I shrugged and looked at the sky with an understanding of the heavy weight of his words. "We all sound like lunatics when it comes to love. I happen to know Sapphira loves your brand of lunacy." I doubted the general needed my words, but that gut feeling brought me out here for a reason. This was all I had to offer the hurting male. A hug wasn't his thing, and I'd wind up with my face in the dirt if I tried.

"You're a good male, Emrys." The words surprised me. I jerked my head in his direction. There was a half-smile on his face. I mentally patted myself on the shoulder.

"Now go somewhere else."

"Yeah." I had helped him by giving him hope. Now he needed space, and I was ready to head back to Dris for a snuggle. I left the wolf staring at his secondary moon and walked back up to the palace and crawled into bed with my softly snoring woman, whose arms pulled me tight. I knew moments like this were short in uncertain times like ours, so I fell asleep with appreciation for every second I had surrounded by the people I cared about most.

Chapter Eighteen

Sapphira

"Thank you." I waved goodbye to the rulers of Asil Tas. Their tan faces smiled at me. They held hands, then arched the free ones to create a large rainbow between them . . . a farewell for a new friend.

Lucky and I had arrived at the mountainous city and were immediately greeted by a tanned-skin man with long brown-hair named Kuanish and his twin sister Kunsulu. They waited patiently in front of their pure white palace with gold domes on three towers shooting up the sides. Somehow Rune's mother had gotten word of my arrival and wishes to the twins before I arrived. As soon as I shifted to Fae and moved to introduce myself, Kaunish interrupted me to tell me they would assist Crysia in battle. Warmth spread over me, and I sensed the truth in their matching brown eyes.

I'd spent the night ready to rest and chat with them but the people of Asil Tas were a lively group. They had a huge party where everyone danced and sang until dawn. I managed to get some sleep, then left with memories of my new friends. My time with them had been fun and sweet yet short. I wished I could have spent more time there, but I was eager to return home.

Now the twins' power over light guided me in the direction of my next stop. Their rainbow twirled in the sky for miles until the edge of their magic faded. One more detour and I'd be on my way to see my mate, my family, and my friends. After we destroyed Verin and the baby was born, I'd love to venture out and spend time with the people of our world.

All thoughts as I soared through the sky shifted to my baby. The little babe was growing like crazy, and my stomach had quite the bump on it. I probably looked around 20 weeks pregnant by human standards. I'd needed to stop and eat more, and my emotions were a bit erratic, but I managed to keep myself from destroying small villages with each irritable shift. Lucky kept close whenever we took a flying break for me to replenish my powers. My little pet had grown a little around the belly as well since we'd connected. Once the fear of him melting people dissipated, everyone who met the stinker spoiled him.

"We should reach Lunnaya Skala in the morning." I held a handful of berries to his snout, and he scooped them all up, leaving drool in the berries' stead.

"I doubt it will be as easy to win over the queen there like it was with the twins but we can cross our fingers, right?" I rubbed my bump gently, and the baby wiggled beneath my hand. I think it was my favorite thing so far about being pregnant—the wiggles.

"Your dad is going to love this." I wanted him here to experience this with me. So close, so damn close. I needed to remind myself that gathering allies was to give us a fighting chance against Verin and potentially the remaining Dramens. Not flying home immediately hurt, but losing everything I cared about would destroy me.

My eyes closed and I thought of my friend's faces. Nyx and Tor were probably arguing one minute, then holding each other in the next. I laughed, then drifted to what Dris and Emrys were possibly doing. No doubt the goat Fae would annoy her, and she'd pretend to hate it but secretly loved having him around. While I distracted myself with thoughts of home, I missed the vibrations of movements on the cool earth. Lucky squealed to alarm me of danger before his eyes grew heavy and his steps wobbled then he collapsed. What the hell happened? A tingle instantly coursed through me as my skin turned hard as diamond, and I readied my powers for an attack.

"Princess Sapphira." A cool voice weaved through the trees on a chilled gust of wind.

"Who's there?" I barreled, sparing a glance at Lucky to see if he still breathed. His little chest moved up and down peacefully despite the potential danger nearby. He remained asleep when I nudged him lightly with my boot.

"I'm a friend or an enemy. All depends." A petite woman with thin, angular white eyes and bluish short hair stepped into my peripheral. A male with dark skin stood beside her, his white eyes watching me cautiously. They were dressed in ornate jeweled finery. Rich blues, silvers, and white crystals sparkled in the light of my fire.

"I'm not in the mood for this." I bit back a growl and surveyed my options. I could grab Lucky and run, but chances are they would catch me since they appeared to be Fae as well. My shifting power hadn't regenerated completely, but I might be able to get a few miles away.

"That is unfortunate. If you wish for aid in the upcoming war against Verin, I need you to do me a favor." Ice rose from her short hair until fifty little spikes decorated her head like a crown. A crown?

"Are you from Lunnaya Skala?" I lowered my hands an inch, hopeful this icy woman knew of the kingdom I searched for. The woman nodded and her companion lowered his hands. Lucky's mouth opened wide with a yawn, then he rolled over, eyes blinking softly at me.

"Verin came to me last week, wishing an alliance between us. My kingdom has escaped his advances and detriment for this long but I fear my kingdom can no longer stay neutral. I will give you the choice before I do what I must to protect my people." She stepped closer, ice coating the ground in her wake. The Ice Queen had greeted me in these quiet woods; this favor of hers must have needed privacy to voice.

"What is the choice?" I dropped my guard completely. If I wanted these people to trust me, then I needed to show I meant them no harm. The queen dropped her head slightly, a recognition of my willingness to listen.

"A precious gem has been taken by the monster in the ice caves up the mountains. Retrieve the gem and I will pledge my allegiance to you." She lifted her hand and a small egg-shaped gem grew in her palm.

"This is a replica so you know what to look for. Its cave has many treasures, and this is all I seek." She dropped it into my hand, and I examined it at every angle.

"If you fail or choose not to accept the quest, I will have no choice but to align my kingdom with Verin's." Her cold words and demeanor caused shivers up my spine. This woman meant every word that dripped from her thin silver lips. As a future queen I understood the need for survival. Whatever this gem was to her, it gave her hope of winning with us. Without it, she would not gamble her people. Verin must have shown her something that gave him an edge over us. I thought through my options and timeline. If I finished this quest quickly, then I could hurry home like planned. However, things rarely went according to plan.

"I take it this quest is dangerous." The queen's unreadable expression caused my stomach to roll.

"Deadly," she purred.

I'd heard of the winter armies of Lunnaya Skala when studying to be queen many years ago. They were ruthless like their queen. They could turn any human into a block of ice in seconds. I didn't know if we could win this war without them, but I knew we couldn't win against them and Verin's soldiers.

"I'll do it." With those words, I sealed the fate of my people and my future on a quest for a gem.

Chapter Nineteen

Sapphira

The mountain's pointed snowy peaks lingered in the gray clouds. They mocked me with their magnificence while I nervously flew higher than ever before. The chill nipped at my body, and I vaguely thought to shift into a snowy owl. However, I suspected the wind up here would toss an owl body around easily. The Ice Queen gave me few details about the ice cave and even less details about the monster who inhabited it. Lucky stayed with the queen until I returned, which was one less thing I had to focus on during this dangerous mission. I'd slept for a few hours, ate a sandwich from my bag to regain my energy, then took off. I figured I'd be able to handle myself as a dragon since not many creatures could fight one off.

I underestimated the cold, and my reptilian body didn't like it. The wind bit into my scales, and I shivered which dropped me several feet in the process. Instinctively, I unleashed a blast of fire in my path and flew through it. The flames warmed me but did not burn. The heat lasted for a few minutes but it was enough for me to make it to the top of the vicious jagged peaks of the mountains. Supposedly, the cave could be seen from above, but the snow and ice looked alike to me. Slowly, I lowered closer to the ground for a different view. The roar of the wind dulled my hearing, but I still listened for the crunching of movement in snow. Nothing.

I flew over the five peaks three times before my frustration got the better of me and I growled loudly. Snow collapsed and fell below my sight. Shit. Hopefully, I hadn't caused a major avalanche. A bright light suddenly caught me off guard, and I squinted, searching for the blinding source. A large patch of thick ice reflected the sun directly at me. That had to be the ice cave I searched for. I dashed toward it and landed softly in three feet deep snow.

Instantly, a large beast with white fur, three big eyes, and a blue snout ran out at me. Fangs bared and two rock-like arms slammed into the snow with every jump toward me. Fire blasted past my pointed teeth. The creature hissed, then took off in the other direction, climbing far away from my blaze. The monster of the cave wasn't that difficult after all. I waited a few minutes in case the beast came back for another round, but it seemed to have known I was the apex predator in our fight. I strode as close to the cave as I could in dragon form, then shifted to Fae. Thankfully, the queen gave me a thicker coat than the one I had brought in my bag. The air hurt as it touched my body. I willed my skin to turn hard as diamonds, hoping to thwart the bitter cold from causing damage. I breathed out into my hands and walked into the smooth and very slippery cave.

However, after two falls on my ass, I grew little sapphire spikes from the bottom of my boots to help navigate the ice without hurting myself. The tunnel delved deep into the mountain, and once the light stopped bouncing off the glistening walls, I lit a ball of fire into my hands to see.

"Come on icy gem. Where are you hiding?" I whispered, and scanned the cuts of the walls or the lack of cuts for a better description. It was if something burned this hole, using the flame to melt rock and smooth the ice in seconds where it stayed perfectly preserved. That beast probably found this cave and made it home. I doubted a creature like it could have done this. But I wouldn't have suspected Lucky of harnessing the power of the sun's radiation, so I could be wrong.

Minutes passed, and a light grew in the distance. I gripped the hilt of the sword I'd carried from Regno Dei Lupi. It had a black blade like all the soldiers in that kingdom . . . like Rune's sword back home. I wondered if that was the only thing he kept from his cruel past there.

The cave opened up into an antechamber, then split into two tunnels. Ice and rock stalactites hung above me, and I lifted onto the balls of my feet. Of course, grabbing the gem wouldn't be easy. I'd have to search both directions until I found the creature's lair of treasure. My eyes scanned every inch of the space for clues as to which way to go. Surely, the beast would have left some mark with their steps, anything to show life within this place. As I neared the tunnel to my right, claw marks carved into the ice floor in the left tunnel caught my attention. I just had to be at the right angle to see them.

"Left tunnel it is," I breathed, ready to be done with this favor. I followed the claw marks with the light of my small fire and grew confused with each step. The lines spun and dipped deep into the ice, like something had been dragged and tried to get away. I shivered, and not from the cold. A light shone ahead and I instantly extinguished my fire. In the depths of my gut, I sensed the beast I'd scared off before didn't live here. Something else did, and it was still inside this cave, eating whatever had carved these marks on the floor. The sound of ripping flesh and wet mouthfuls of meat hit my sensitive hearing. Something purred as it devoured its meal. The scent of coopery blood mixed with rot hit my nose, and I almost threw up. My stomach churned and a wave of nausea rolled through me.

"Not now baby, we've got to make it through this," I mentally said to the baby. Slowly, I pulled my blade from it scabbard. I moved as silently as possible and crouched and peered around the edge of the tunnel. Another antechamber contained piles upon piles of gold, precious gems, and a variety of jewelry. The treasures sat on the rocks and ice. A large flat boulder stood in the middle of the trove and on it sat a monster even my nightmares couldn't conjure. White skin with blue-and-black freckles scattered across its elongated human-like body. Pointed fingers dug into the skin of a large white bear as it bit into the exposed meat, chewing and licking the blood from the muscles. Its eyes closed in rapture from the meal. A long tail twitched with each bite and glimmers of ice stuck out from its head and back. I'd forever be haunted by the sight of this demon. Surely, this thing had come from the depths of hell and not of this magical realm.

As it ate, I analyzed the room for the damn egg. If I could just get closer, maybe I could shoot first to kill the demon and then search for it. My stomach rolled again as I took a step closer. The baby did not like this scenario, and I agreed. The scent was going to be the death of my insides if I didn't get out of here quickly. I rapidly breathed in and out through my mouth, hoping to give my nose a break. As I inhaled and exhaled the nausea calmed and my body relaxed. My gaze shifted from the treasure to the demon again and I gasped.

I was wrong earlier. Its eyes hadn't been closed while savoring the bloody carcass. It didn't have eyes. A large triangular-shaped hole where its nose should be wiggled as it sniffed the air; bloody rows upon rows of sharp teeth snarled while two pointed ears twisted in multiple directions. Crap. My mouth-breathing caught its attention. Note to self: Never mouth-breath in dangerous situations.

Suddenly, the demon twisted its head in an unnatural way in my direction. It sniffed the air and a rattling noise echoed from its chest across the room. The dead animal dropped to the floor and the thing rose onto its haunches, the long tail behind it swirling around tauntingly. I shook my arms and readied myself for a fight.

Time for this princess to send a demon back to hell.

Chapter Twenty

Sapphira

I stepped into the open antechamber and waited for the beast to run at me. Its nose hole wiggled as it sniffed for me; the eyeless holed head shifted with each of my steps. The demon knew exactly where I was in the room.

"What are you waiting for?" I bellowed, tired of waiting for it to attack. A mixture of blood and drool fell from its teeth before it vanished completely.

"Shit." I cursed and scanned the room, on guard for it to reappear in the most frightening way. Taking advantage of the eerie situation, I took off to weave around the piles of treasure. If I could find that damn egg, then I could collapse the room and hopefully the demon within it. After two passing rounds, I hadn't spied the creature or the egg. But I knew they were here somewhere.

Trying something different, I jumped and stomped the ground once before continuing to run around with my sword ready to slice. The ground shook and the treasure rattled loudly. The sides collapsed like an avalanche. New gold and valuables were exposed, and that's when I saw it. A blue egg-shaped gem sat inside a black crown with rubies on top of the pile nearest me. I leaped up and reached to grab the gem when my boot slipped on some loose gold coins. I twisted and fell flat on my back. Drool dripped onto my wincing face and the demon appeared directly above me on the roof of the chamber. Its jaw opened wider than my head and a forked tongue hissed as it released its grip on the ice. Falling, falling. I lifted my sword for it to impale but it vanished seconds before touching the sharp blade. Fingers wrapped around my ankle and tossed me against the wall.

Instantly, teeth bared in front of my face as it roared. Without remorse, I threw up. The stench of the beast finally took its toll, and I couldn't think of a more lifesaving moment. My body heaved onto the icy jeweled floor while the creature clawed at its face to get the stench and debris of my stomach off. My stomach ached and the burning in my throat was near crippling, but I crawled to my feet anyway. The demon's long tail whipped my back and I crashed into the wall. I mentally thanked my powers and the diamond skin protecting me and the baby. Arms wrapped around me and teeth scraped at my neck in an attempt to rip my head off. Sounds of bones scraping against my hardened skin echoed in my ear and the demon screamed as it tried to gnaw me and couldn't find a weak spot. My powers held for now, but in time my body would become soft enough to be shredded across the ice.

I closed my eyes and imagined my body turning to a living flame. When I opened my lids, everything glowed with a reddish tinge. The demon released me, and I ran to seize the gem. Claws scraped at my back as I moved, a large tail whipped into my view, and I rolled across the ground then hopped back up. I jumped onto the trove and clenched the palm-sized gem in my hand. It weighed more than I would have suspected but tucked it in close while I eyed the way out. The demon screamed and hopped onto my back. We collapsed amongst the gold and jewels.

"I am not going to be buried in a fucking treasure trove, you demon!" I screamed and threw my head back, slamming into its skull. It released me, and I scrambled away, thinking I might become a dragon right now. I tossed fire around me as I ran into the tunnel exit. I heard the thing run after me, and I slammed my hand against a patch of rock on the wall. The icy channel vibrated as earth splintered all around us. I'd struck a match to this mountain and if I didn't get out in time, it would burn me with the demon.

I pushed, harder and harder, faster and faster. My lungs burned for more air and my muscles threatened to cramp. It felt like I lifted boulders instead of my legs. I forced myself up the dark tunnel with the sound of the demon behind me. I flung a fireball back to slow it down, but I didn't succeed. The ice cracked beneath my feet, and the mountain shook. I was running out of time. "Almost there, almost there," I repeated over and over as I saw the light of the snowy air outside. Ice broke apart and the rock began to open up ahead. Shit. Pure desperation to get out of here led me to shift. I gripped the gem tightly in my hands as my bones broke and the creature flew past me to escape his doomed lair. The tunnel was snug against my dragon body but I released my fire to widen the ice and ran. My legs covered more distance, leaving the demon in my wake. Its claws tried to find a way to sink into my scales but found no such advantage.

The cool fresh air welcomed me as I shot into the sky and turned just as the demon found the exit. Flame and snow mixed as I torched that horrid creature and its cursed mountain. Rock crumbled and the mountain broke apart, stone and snow tumbling down its steep slopes. The sounds of the demon meeting its doom were the perfect ending to this adventure as I flapped my wings twice, then flew toward the waiting queen of Lunnaya Skala.

The city appeared to be carved of ice with a large square wall around the palace and smaller dwellings. People screamed as they saw a dragon in the sky but I only had eyes for the white figure standing in front of the palace with a little dot racing around it. My little Lucky was eager to see me. I landed in the winter land courtyard of white trees with icicles hanging from their branches. The palace shook as I landed, and I turned into my Fae self. I wanted to throw the damn gem at her cold face.

"Well done." She held out her hand, and I limped over to drop it into her waiting palm. The adrenaline wore off and aches blossomed inside my body.

"I need food, and I need sleep," I groaned as I dropped to my knees and Lucky touched his snout to my hand for attention.

"Hey buddy." I winced as pain shot through my shoulder where the demon had gnawed on me.

"I have a room prepared for you with various foods. Rest now, Princess Sapphira, conqueror of the Nevidimy Led." She dropped her free-gloved hand to me, and I grasped it tightly. One step at a time, she guided me into the spiky ice palace.

"Was that thing really worth facing that demon?" I grumbled, and the queen nodded.

"I will show you before your departure." She walked me up surprisingly textured ice stairs to a hall with many doors. I sighed and my body was close to collapsing. That battle with the demon wore me out and the baby was claiming all the energy I had left.

"You are safe here. No one will harm you." She opened a door, and helped me into a lavish room with blue rugs covering the floor and a stone fireplace with a hot flame dancing inside. A massive bed with thick white blankets beckoned me.

"Rest, dear one. You've earned it." I released her hand and climbed into the bed. My powers and body were drained. I barely noticed the queen click her tongue and Lucky followed her out of the room before sleep claimed me.

Chapter Twenty-One

Sapphira

After sleeping for four hours, I woke up starving. The queen had mentioned food, so I rolled over to find it. In front of a floor-to-ceiling window stood a large table with a dozen covered plates on it. Moonlight coated them so they were probably all cold dishes by now, but I didn't care. Slowly, I moved off the bed and sat in the fur-covered chair next to the food. My body still ached, mostly in my back and legs, but thankfully my hard skin had protected me. If not, I would have refused the quest for the queen's favor to protect the baby.

"How are you doing, little one?" I rubbed my slightly larger bump and opened the lids to the various dishes. Fruit, cheeses, breads, and hot soup greeted me. Maybe they exchanged the soup for hot ones for me recently, I thought to myself. The cheese looked delicious so I tore into that first. The baby moved around joyously after a few minutes of eating, and I hoped that meant a happy baby. I placed my hand a few inches above my stomach and released the healer's power from Aminthe to double-check the babe's health. The tiny heartbeat pulsed in my hands strongly and rhythmically. A feeling of safety warmed my mind. No hurt bones or organs, as far as I could tell. The diamond skin did its job protecting the most precious part of me.

Once I ate my fill, I cleaned myself in the hot shower. Inside the bathroom hung two dresses, one bluish-gray and the other white. Both looked warm and comfortable versus lavish. I tried on the bluish one, which had thick, long sleeves and a ribbon that tied around my waist, allowing it to flow freely to my feet. I liked that the dress left plenty of room for the bump underneath the fabric. Slippers with fur on the inside waited by the door to slip on as I departed the room.

I wanted to go home so badly, but I had to make sure everything was fine here before leaving again. The Ice Queen was a mystery to me, and I sensed there was more to her than the cold expression she wore so well. The few people I passed in the halls bowed their heads before continuing on their paths, and one showed me the direction to the queen when asked. She sat in the throne room, with the guard I'd met before at her side. Ten women in white armor and fur cloaks stood in front of her. I'd walked in on a meeting of sorts.

"Princess Sapphira, please join us." The queen motioned for me to enter before I could mutter apologies for intruding. A chair out of ice formed at her side, and her guard placed a pillow from behind her own icy throne for me to sit upon.

"My elite warriors and war council." She gestured to the women standing at attention. Their bodies ranged in size and height. Their skins were all a shade of white with various pastels blended in. No matter the color or length of their hair, each strand was twisted into locs. They breathed power and strength behind their bright armor.

"Nice to meet you." I waved and one of the shortest ladies with pastel-pink hair waved back with a grin.

"We were discussing our departure for Crysia; the safest route to take will be by sea. To go by land will mean passing Verin's territory."

I'd planned to stick to the coast after crossing the straight for the same reason. A squeal echoed across the open throne room, and Lucky leaped into view. Three of the guards squatted down to pet my little attention seeker as he strutted by.

"You've spoiled him." I smirked and the queen's lips lifted, then shrugged in a nonroyal way.

"Now that you have awoken, it's time to rally my people, then prepare to send you off the Lunnayian warrior way." She stood and cradled the egg gem in her hands as she walked to the two large doors on our right. I followed behind, as did the warriors. Lucky leaped into a guard's arms, and she carried him with pride behind us.

119

With a wave of her free hand, the doors slowly opened to a large balcony. The cold air brushed against me, but the thick dress kept the chill away. Cautiously, I glanced over the end of the spiked railing to see no one stood beneath like I would have expected. How could she rally her people when her people didn't know she stood here?

She held the gem up between her hands toward the moon above and then peeled her fingers away at the same time. I winced, waiting for the thing to fall on her head but it stayed there, floating between her hands like magic. I waited for something to happen.

Minutes passed by and it continued to float between her perfectly manicured hands. I glanced at the guards around me, but they all stared at the egg. A bright light caught my attention as the egg glowed. It vibrated in the air, and a beam shot from the moon to the gem while tiny snowflakes dropped from its rounded sides. Everyone was silent, waiting for something to happen with awe written on their faces. Suddenly, the glowing stopped and the queen floated the gem down to chest level. Ice grew from the queen's hands, wrapped around it, then it glowed again. Her hands disconnected from the ice only to form a pedestal of sorts to cradle it.

"Crack!" The sound echoed across the land as a large fissure formed on the side of the gem. One of the guards fell to her knees, hands covering her gaped mouth.

"I can't believe it," another mumbled and I struggled to understand what they saw.

"Crack!" Another line grew on the gem. Suspense gripped hold of my mind. In the time it took to exhale, the gem shattered. The diamond power rushed over my skin to protect the baby from any debris.

"Welcome to the world, we've been waiting a long time for you." The queen's calm voice softened further, and I gasped at the sight on the pedestal. A small blue bird, with icy feathers lay inside.

"The ice phoenix has long been a symbol for my people. The last one disappeared the day Verin's poison stretched across the land. I'd searched for many years and found nothing of their existence again, until one of my people saw the Nevidimy Led raiding a nest, then carrying the last egg to its lair. Many tried to retrieve it, but none prevailed." She gently stroked the side of the bird as it lay in the ice, chirping, and tried to open its eyes.

"Verin is afraid of you. I knew nothing about you, Princess, besides that . . . which is all I needed to know. This fact told me you would be the one to bring hope back to my kingdom. And you did by bringing this magnificent creature back to us. You have my gratitude and my armies, Princess of Crysia." She tipped her head and the guards bowed beside me.

"What a precious moment." That voice . . . so familiar, so irritating. Everyone on the balcony shifted to the throne room behind us where my cousin, Lethirya, stood against the icy throne her father sat upon.

"You've made your decision, then," he stated while picking at something on his fingernail. The queen stood in front of the phoenix and her guard stood in front of her, white bows and swords readied to attack.

"It has been decided," the queen announced, her fingers snuck between us to lace with mine. I absorbed some of her powers naturally, but then I felt a surge of ice within my veins. The queen was giving me more. She must have known about my gifts and wanted Verin to know that I now processed a fraction of them, too. His golden eyes narrowed at our connection.

"Shame." His eyes roamed over me, then stared at the apparent baby bump. Instinctually, I tried to block my baby from his gaze with my hands.

"Interesting twist, Little Gem. A new prize has entered this marvelous game between us," he purred, his evil stare locked onto my belly. Dread coated my insides at the thought of him anywhere near my child.

Faster than a viper, the queen threw sharp icicles at Lethirya and Verin. However, they were already walking through a portal. Her ice embedded deep in the throne and walls behind it. I tried not to let the encounter with Verin get to me, but that icky feeling inside refused to budge. A new prize, he had stated. I focused on my breaths as alarms went off in my head. My child would be born with the power of the Heart Tree. Life, death, and magic will run through her tiny heart. Verin sensed this. Somehow.

"I've got to get home," I announced, and the queen nodded.

"Yes, let us prepare you for your departure."

Chapter Twenty-Two

Rune

After the attack, the queen and I decided the diamond wall would remain. Verin's skirmish had been a test to see how our defenses were going. Crysia won, but his forces got farther than they should have.

"Never gets easier." Desmire spoke from my left side. The dragon had helped burn the dead on the altars I had lifted from the ground. Crysia's burial site sat a mile from the palace on the side of a mountain. The fire had long disappeared, but I watched as the black earth turned green, then sprouted the white-and-pink flowers called unity stars. They were no bigger than a thumbnail with six pointed petals. They only grew on burial sites, especially after the ground was set aflame. Death united everyone in the end. No one has determined why these flowers grace our dead, but I'm grateful for their presence.

"It doesn't," I agreed and once the entire field blossomed with the precious flower, I headed for home.

"Any updates on my daughter?" the dragon asked, his long steps catching up to me in seconds.

"She's fine. I don't always hear her when I focus but two days ago she was muttering about cheese and agreeing with the babe that the soup was good. If she can eat soup and cheese, then I know she is safe." It's odd how the thought of cheese comforts me so much. My mate is somewhere alive, with sustenance. I know she is on her way back to me and her kingdom. If I searched for her, I may find her, but instinct told me to be patient. I'd see my mate soon.

"She's stubborn and headstrong like her mother. And me." He laughed.

I shook my head. The man had been helpful since showing up on the battle at Crystoria. He didn't speak as much as Tor or Emrys did. He treated me as a son to be proud of. His gray eyes constantly crinkled with approval when I jumped into action as general. The unfamiliar feeling left me both unsure and honored. As we made our way to the palace, the air seemed electric. A joyous buzz jumped from the trees to the grass, to the rocks, then back to the air. Something was happening. I closed my eyes and listened as Desmire did the same.

"You feel that?" I asked, knowing the dragon was older and had been one with the land as an animal for twenty years. My beast vibrated, and I tried to quiet him down to hear what the buzz was about.

"Dragonnn," the wind whispered, over and over.

"Dragonnnnn," it called, but as I looked at the dragon shifter beside me, I felt none of the buzz around him.

"I knew it," he whispered, and departed quickly to the palace. I raced after him, trailing behind by about four feet. I frequently looked up at the sky, as if a sign would fall from the clouds.

"Something's coming." Dris ran into the garden just as we arrived.

"She's here," Desmire's voice echoed with awe, and the queen arrived at his side moments later. She? I searched the skies as Desmire did and shifted constantly, desperate to see what he saw. A shadow grew over the setting sun's light, then a large black-and-blue dragon flew over us.

"I can't believe it." Dris burst into tears as the dragon circled the palace. My heart thundered and my body grew light as if I could take off and fly, too. My mate. My mate had come home. More guards, Nyx, and Tor joined us on the grass as Sapphira lowered her dragon body. A creature jumped from her claws and ran around the garden excitedly. Light flashed, and in the glow, the dragon grew smaller, more human-like.

"Sapphira." Her mother cried and raced to her daughter as she appeared before us, perfect and beautiful as the last day I had seen her.

Sapphira's eyes filled with tears. Her hair, twisted in locs, draped over her white armor, which allowed room for her small, rounded belly. My moon had come back to me. I didn't move, afraid if I breathed too hard, if I moved an inch, I would be prone to taking her away from everyone to show her how badly I missed her. She was hugged and greeted with smiles and tears from nearly all in the garden. People congratulated her on the baby and welcomed her home. She searched the crowd until our gazes collided. Mine.

More tears flowed onto her cheeks as her lips parted. She was real and safe and here. My knees trembled but I stood strong. She hugged her family and friends, but her gaze belonged to me. Slowly, she walked over and my beast howled within.

"Rune," she whispered reverently. Her hand caressed my scared cheek and a rushed breath flew past my lips.

"I'm home," she whispered, like she couldn't believe the words herself. The hold I placed on my body broke. I pulled her to me and touched all of her before I cradled that beautiful face and kissed her lips.

"I missed you," she sobbed with a smile on her face, as I kissed her with every ounce of longing I'd endured. Blinding need seared my essence . . . the need to take care of my mate overrode all other thought. I scooped her up and raced into the palace to her room. Nyx had kept everything in order, and I set

127

my mate on the bed gently. She smirked as I leaned over to place my hands on her stomach. She'd grown so much in our time apart. I'd missed watching the baby grow, but I would miss no more.

"You gave me as much time as you could with my family, didn't you?" She chuckled and the sound caused a growl to erupt from my chest.

"They can have you later. Right now, you're mine."

She shivered. Her hands roamed through my hair, my jaw, then down my chest.

"Much, much later." She leaned closer to whisper against my lips, and I lost control.

Chapter Twenty-Three

Sapphira

Rune's kiss soothed every part of me that had been on edge since my cousin had dumped me in the desert. I felt whole with every breath of him. His hands gently ripped at the buckles of the Lunnayian armor across my torso.

"Never again," he growled, the armor tossed over his shoulder.

"I'll try not to get kidnapped again." I smiled as his hot mouth kisses traveled down my neck, teeth nipping at my ear. He growled again and I gripped at his hair. I loved it when this man growled for me. He was the rock that kept me grounded. My steadfast and gorgeous mate. I clawed at the gray tunic covering his muscled chest. I wanted to touch him, to see the realness of his body before me. This wasn't a dream; I could taste him on my tongue, feel the flex of his powerful arms under my fingers. He gripped me like he feared I'd disappear. Silently, we removed every fabric that clung to our bodies. When lips weren't connected, our gazes were. I needed my mate like this, and I knew he needed it, too.

"Is it safe to . . .?" His hands cradled the baby bump so softly, and I bit my lip. His concern for hurting me while pregnant melted me more than I'd thought possible. This warrior had bathed in the blood of enemies, scared nearly every person that met him, and here he sat bowed in reverence to our child.

"I ran into a healer in Regno Dei Lupi that said we could do our thing. The baby is essentially in a little swimming pool. Completely safe." I'd blurted the question to Aminthe before leaving and she laughed while telling me great positions for when my stomach grew larger. Rune's hands stilled and his eyes narrowed on my face.

"Do you wanna talk about it now?" I asked, knowing he may want to put this moment on hold to discuss my journey. If he did, I would understand. I just wouldn't be liable if I lunged for him in inappropriate settings later. Seeing his battle-shaped body and smelling his sandalwood and waterfall scent drove my senses wild. He remained unmoving for multiple steady breaths, then shook his head.

"Later. I have time to make up for." He lowered himself to his knees, eyes on mine as he bent between my legs at the edge of the bed. He whispered so low that I couldn't hear what he said to our child. He pressed a long kiss to my stomach. For however long I lived, I would never forget this moment. His tenderness, his love, his bright heart radiated with every touch and look he gave me.

"I love you." My hands ran through his black hair, which had grown since the last time I had seen

130

him. He looked like he'd been through hell. He lowered his head to the apex of my thighs. My fingers on top his head tightened at the first caress of his tongue.

"Rune," I moaned as he started slow, then increased his devouring of me.

"I missed hearing my name on your tongue." The vibrations of his voice brought me closer to rapture. Each suck, nibble, and lick wrecked pleasure throughout my senses. I tensed as the sudden release tore through me. Ripples of shivers danced up and down my nerves. He lifted his head, and my heart raced. Rune's face was positively predatory. His hands gripped my hips and they slid off the bed with a yank, only to be cradled in his strong hold. I fell back onto my elbows, taking in the sight of him before me. Bulging pecs and tensed abdominal muscles flexed as he prodded my entrance.

"Look at me," he demanded and I did. Slowly, he pushed into me and my hooded eyes tried to focus on his face.

"Rune," I breathed, watching as his lips parted with every thrust. I nearly lost it at the sight of him fully connected, hips pressed to hips.

"Rune." His name echoed in the room, a mixture of moans and pleading. The sounds snapped something in him. He unleashed himself upon my defenseless body. I gripped the mattress as he held my legs hostage to his relentless pounding. The prince showed me with every ounce of his body how much he had missed me. My legs were thrown over his shoulders and his hands gripped my breasts, fingers teasing me.

"Oh, Rune!" I screamed as I dug my heels into his shoulders, toes curled as earth-shattering waves of ecstasy crashed over me. My moans shifted to whimpers as he upped his pace and the cusps of another release threatened me.

"What do you think, mate, one orgasm for every day separated?" He grinned, and I scrambled to pull his lips to mine. He saw the need in my eyes. Quickly, he withdrew from me and dropped my legs. With my body secured in his arms, he lifted me onto the middle of the bed. He was so strong as he crawled over me, hips settling between my thighs while being careful enough to leave room for the bump. Our lips connected, and I cried into his mouth as he slid into my needy sex, his focus solely on the long and hard thrusts to drive me senseless. Every inch of those long strokes pulling out then pushing back inside me made me whimper his name.

"Rune . . ."

"Rune . . ."

"Rune . . ."

"I never stopped believing I'd see you again, I never stopped craving your touch, your smile that always brings me to my damn knees." My mate poured out his soul and I gripped his arms, my hips lifting to bring me closer to him.

"I can't lose you," he whispered. His words broke with a hitched breath. He ceased moving his hips, and I glanced up to see tears brimming in his eyes. I cradled his face.

Matching tears spilled onto my cheeks as I searched for the words to soothe his suffering. "You will never lose me. I will always, always return to you. I will always feel you, always fight to be with you. In this life, and every one after that." I vowed nothing could keep me from him forever. His lips smashed against mine as our worlds collided in a clash of tongue and teeth. His tears mixed with mine as they fell to the sheets.

"I'm here," I breathed into him, knowing he needed to hear it as much as I did.

"Together." He groaned and ground himself into me, his head at my neck, teeth sinking into my skin. Our moans rattled the walls as I came again, his release joining me. Together. He rolled us over, my sweat-covered body draped over his.

"That was . . ." I gasped; my breathing hadn't slowed yet. "A lot . . ." It was a lot. Everything ached in the most delicious ways.

"I love you, Sapphira." His hand rubbed my back and I purred. I'd never tire of this man, we were mates, created for each other, and I needed him at my side. I lifted off him to go to the bathroom, then sleepily climbed into bed. The journey here and Rune's intense reunion sex had exhausted me.

"Sleep, I'll be here when you wake up and all the days after." He held me as I snuggled into his chest, breathing in our mingled scents. Rune's voice soothed me to sleep, reminding me that I had done it. I made it home and into the arms of my mate. Safe. Me and the babe were safe.

For now.

Chapter Twenty-Four

Dris

"I can't believe you met the legendary Ice Queen of Lunnaya Skala." My hands covered my open mouth. After Rune had whisked Sapphira away, we didn't see her until the morning when she joined us for breakfast. Mates needed time to bond after long separations, so we understood it. We all sat in the gardens with a feast of a breakfast while Sapphira shared the details about her journey. Emrys played with Lucky while I fought the desire to ink her story to paper. She'd visited three kingdoms that Crysia had lost touch with twenty years ago.

"She was everything you think an Ice Queen would be, and her top guards are all women. So badass," Sapphira gushed, then nibbled on some strawberries. She'd changed so much since I had last seen her . . . not only from the babe in her belly, but her hair styled in the signature Lunnayian locs of the guards and her demeanor. No longer a lost human or growing princess, she sat with the confidence of a queen. She had fought through her situation, pressed on, and gained allies along the way.

"That is one kingdom I did not get to venture into. So cold." Queen Olyndria feigned a shiver and her mate, who sat beside her, huffed. They'd been happy to sit with us younger folk and relish in the happy reunion.

"But Asil Tas always had the best fashion," Nyx chimed in.

I'd seen these places in the books of the library but never in person. Now I wanted to see them with my own big eyes. Emrys would join me, of course. The opportunity for him to cause mischief would be too great to ignore.

"That's cool and all but, I would have sold my essence to see father's face when you cracked the throne room's floor. He must have been so pissed." Tor laughed and Rune smirked, his hand squeezing Sapphira's shoulder. There hadn't been a foot between them since they had come down from her room. Sapphira giggled with Tor and nodded.

"He sucks, but your mom is nice. She somehow convinced the twins at Asil Tas to join us before I arrived." The princess reached her hand over to Rune's knee and squeezed twice. The flirtation between those two mates had everyone attempting to revert their gazes more than a few times.

"You made Crysia proud. Allies will help us greatly when Verin comes. My sources show he has thousands at his command, waiting and growing in the badlands. He will have convinced the Dramens to join him after the defeat at Crystoria. You will make a great queen, my daughter."

Sapphira smiled at her mom and lifted one of the diamond tea cups for a toast. "I'm glad to be home. I love you all." Tears rolled down her uplifted cheeks. We enjoyed sharing the smiles and laughter .. . Sapphira was safe. We desperately needed a moment like this. Everything seemed to move so quickly that we've barely had a break to breathe. I knew life would continue to get complicated with allies en route to Crysia, the war, and a baby on the way. There was so much to do, which made moments like this precious. I pushed away thoughts of tomorrow and focused on the now.

"So, now that everyone is here, I have something I wanna do," Tor breathed with his hands in his pockets. Nyx eyed him suspiciously, as he faced her.

"If any of this has taught me one thing, it's that we have to live the life we want in the time that we have. Nyx, we're still figuring this mate thing out, but I know I don't want to wait any longer to call you my wife. You are stubborn, you are so damn resilient, and strong-willed. But more than any of your finer traits, you are the perfect companion for me. I wish I'd seen it sooner, but everything that happened led me right to you." He pulled a beautiful blue turquoise ring with diamonds around the band out of his pocket. "My mate, will you marry me?"

Nyx's body went completely still. Nobody at our picnic dared breathed as we waited for her answer. Tor batted his long eyelashes lovingly and that seemed to snap Nyx out of her shock.

"It's so soon," she whispered, her gaze darting to all of our faces, panic settling in. Tor, bless him, didn't waver. He didn't show signs of rejection; he knew his mate liked to control everything. What he said was right; we only have the time that's given to us, and we have to choose how we live it. Planning, trying to control the uncontrollable, or just drop our oars on this river of life to see where it goes.

"It is, but soon is all we have right now. Years down the road is not a promise either of us can make. In this moment, I am in love with your control freak tendencies, and I am willing to dare that part of you to be right here, with me, and agree to be my wife. Don't forget to think of the beautiful dress you could design. Plus, there is event planning." Tor teased her now, attempting to lighten the mood like he always did. Nyx's lips lifted. His teasing challenge danced like fire tendrils in her purple irises.

He knew the buttons to push, a gift only a soul mate could possess. I glanced at Emrys, who was petting the pig, his attention on the couple then shifting to me. I don't know if we were mates, and honestly, I didn't care if we weren't. I loved him, and he loved me, that was enough. I didn't want anyone other than that goat Fae to annoy me and share in life's surprises.

"So, what do you think, Nyx?" he prodded her once last time. His smile showed all the love and enjoyment he had for her.

"Well since you dared me . . ." she teased back and Tor hugged her, his lips sealing the deal. Joyous laughter echoed around the garden. Once Tor released his future bride, he slid the ring on her finger—a perfect fit. Sapphira and I ran to her at the same time as Rune and Emrys gave Tor a congratulatory nod.

"I'm so happy for you!" I hugged her on one side, and Sapphira wrapped her arms around us from the opposite.

"I can't wait to see what dress you design." Sapphira squeezed us, and I decided we all were living the best life, surrounded by friends celebrating happy change. We gabbed about the future wedding, well after the sun had set, not sparing any of the details. The queen and Desmire eventually left to handle kingdom stuff, already agreeing to whatever Nyx wanted. Food was delivered to us as we lazily enjoyed being united again.

"Despite the troubled times ahead, I'm glad we have these moments together." Sapphira smiled, her body leaning against her mate's chest. Emrys gathered me in his arms and I kissed his cheek and touched his horns with a wink. He hugged me tightly, and I had never felt safer.

"I think it's time for bed," I whispered in his ear, then nibbled his earlobe to get the point across. In true Fae male fashion, Emrys held me in his arms as he stood and rushed to the palace without saying goodbye to our friends. Nyx laughed and I briefly saw Sapphira wave before we disappeared inside.

Chapter Twenty-Five

Emrys

"I'm happy for you." Sapphira slid up to my side, taking a break from helping Nyx with the party plans. The happy couple didn't care to waste time with a long engagement. They'd officially be wed in three days after the proposal. I didn't see it as rushed since the both of them were so stubborn that once a decision was made, they refused to procrastinate.

"I'm happy for you and little Runira, too," I teased, and the princess choked. My barked laugh echoed around the throne room, eyes of the small gathering turning in my direction.

"Runira?"

"Rune and Sapphira put together for a girl's name. I thought about Sapphune, but that didn't sound as pretty. If it's a boy, then Emry." I grinned and felt a familiar set of eyes on me. I glanced at Dris. I liked that she watched me, even if she tried to hide it. We may have been opposites in personality, but I saw my match in her the first time she rolled her eyes. Beneath that librarian lay a curious and adventurous side.

"No!" Rune's growling voice entered the room, and he strode up to Sapphira's side, wrapping his arms around her waist, hands resting on the evidence of their love.

"Oh, I don't know, Rune. Runira is different. A unique name for a unique baby." She winked at me and Rune ignored her. He whispered in her ear and I tuned it out to give them privacy.

"Emrys, can you come here, please?" My little bird waved me over, and I slid up to her in seconds. She looked so beautiful with her wild hair and green ankle-length dress. Her pink cheeks gave her thoughts away. While we didn't have sex last night, we did get very familiar with each other's body with our tongues and hands. The sounds she had made had me questioning my existence. Did I have a life before Dris?

"Dris, you naughty librarian. I didn't know you were into that." It took a few seconds, but Dris realized what I insinuated and rolled her eyes. She shook her head but the pink in her cheeks became bright red. Interesting. I stood at the crossroads of a decision, a daring challenge or let it go. My hand shot out and grabbed hers to set the pen and notes onto a table. I've always found the bolder choices led to sweeter satisfaction. She eyed me cautiously and rightfully so. I had very nefarious thoughts about her right now. I took a step back, her hand in mine, a decision that lay fully with her now. Come play with me, trust me, or stay. She knew I would support either decision.

She glanced to the side, then took a step in my direction. This was why I loved her. She would play with me. Reserved on the outside but oh-so-fiery on the inside. Instantly, I turned us invisible. Being an owl Fae, the sense of freedom came easier for her, especially now that she could fly again. My arms flexed and she came closer.

"Are we . . .?" she whispered and I winked, my finger lifted to my lips to signal silence. Her eyes widened as I leaned in to kiss her softly. She was hard against my lips, being so public had her nervous but a few pecks later, she melted. My lips grinned as her hunger grew, hands gripping at my neck. Swiftly, I picked her up to carry her somewhere a little more private. As soon as we exited the throne room, her tongue flicked my piercing, then hot kisses covered my neck. I groaned, and she shook with restrained laughter.

"I thought we were supposed to be silent." Her hands now pulled the hem of my shirt out of my pants. Her touch seared me, and I gave up trying to make it to either of our rooms. The hallway we stood in appeared deserted for now. There were little windows with billowing white curtains leading to a staircase at the end of the hallway. I tucked into one of the window alcoves. My eyes met with hers.

"As long as you are touching me, you're invisible." She had to understand how this worked if we were going to play around without being seen. Her lip pulled between her teeth and she nodded. Good little bird. My lips returned to hers, and I craved everything she wanted to give. Soft caresses against my abs flexed my hips closer and her legs tightened around my waist. Her fingernails scraped my skin lightly, and I clenched my teeth to keep from moaning. My fingers fiddled with the front ties of her dress. I dropped my head and pressed kisses to the handful and sucked her into my mouth. Now it was her turn to fight back her sweet whimpers. Her hips ground against mine, and I lifted her slightly up, then down, creating an incredible friction for the both of us.

"Wanna head to the gardens tomorrow and pick flowers with me? I wanted to give them to Nyx as a gift from us maids." Two women entered the hall, completely oblivious to us. I froze, but not my Dris. The adventurous side of her had come to play and I fell in love with her even more. That steadfast hand of hers dipped into my pants and palmed me twice, then squeezed. My lips lunged for hers, tongue diving to taste her as she touched me. The two ladies ascended the stairs as she fumbled with the belt and pants that kept me contained. Once released, she reached to her thighs around my waist to shift her dress higher and higher, exposing pastel green panties.

"Dris?" I know I said to keep quiet, but I had to hear her say it.

"I love you, and I want you right now. You bring out this side of me that wants to experience everything. I trust you to keep me safe, while I learn to color outside the lines." Even though I could whisper like she did, my mouth wouldn't move, so I simply nodded. She pulled her panties to the side with one finger and guided me to her with the others. She was ready and wanted this as much as I did. As soon as her hands released their grip on me, I pinned her to the wall beside the window with a quick thrust of my hips. Pure fucking bliss. Our fingers intertwined above her head as she purred.

She wiggled against me, and I pulled back slow and teasingly. Her lips slammed against mine and refused to hold back anymore. We'd have time to draw out each sensation later, right now we played a sinful game and could be caught if the right people walked by. My fingers tightened around hers as I rolled my hips. She breathed into me, then pinched her lips together. My head dropped to her neck as I picked up the pace. Each thrust pounded her into the wall like the finest piece of art I'd ever seen. I thought many times that she was perfect for me. But when her head dipped down to watch our joining, I nearly lost it. Right then I felt it . . . that unshakable bond . . . proof of my theory all along. Dris was more than my match. She was my mate.

Tears leaked from her eyes as she realized the meaning of this feeling, too. I kissed her, deeply, and she reciprocated with need. I know I am a jackass most of the time. You can't be shut down as much as I have and feel worthy all the time. But this . . . this proved what I knew all along. I was worthy of this perfect being. Shivers shot up my spine and I tensed. Her fingers gripped mine as her legs squeezed my hips. She bit my lip once and a sound seeped from her as she found release. I sealed my mouth to hers and drank in the sound as my own ecstasy chased hers.

"So damn beautiful." I kissed her twice, then reached down to secure my pants. She sighed dreamily as I started walking on quiet feet toward her room. Voices echoed from the end of the hallway and Dris giggled against my ear. We made it without being caught, but still had to get to her room without being noticed. With that challenge between us, I raced up the stairs as fast as I could. Once inside, she climbed off me and walked to the bathroom. I heard the water being turned on and got excited for a bath. My lips lifted as a naked Dris walked out and I stalked forward. Here's to living adventurously with my mate.

Chapter Twenty-Six

Sapphira

Crysia buzzed with the excitement of the wedding. Nyx planned an elegant ceremony in the gardens, then a party in the throne room where most balls were hosted. Tor didn't care what happened as long as the night ended with marriage.

A smile had been permanently fixed on my face since I arrived home. Lucky had made himself comfortable, too. At first, Rune didn't approve of him sleeping in the room with us. But he quickly became the first one to greet the creature with a smile and cuddle. Such a spoiled little thing. I'm glad he came with me; I don't know how I would have made it on my own without talking to him. He gave me something to look after besides myself and the babe. I needed that. Nightmares of being tossed into the desert tried to disrupt my sleep at night, but Rune whispered to remind me that I was home.

Everything had changed and would change more with every passing hour. The babe continued to grow, and Rista predicted the baby would be full grown in a few weeks. I ignored thoughts of Verin's impending war most likely coinciding around the same timeframe. He was interested in my baby, possibly because he knew of the Heart Tree's essence swirling inside her. I'd sooner cut his head off than let him get close enough to touch my baby.

"You frown like your mother." A deep voice resonated beside me and I looked up to see my father. The unexpected frown he mentioned vanished, and I hugged him when he sat on the bench beside me.

"Got lost in thought." His eyebrow arched. My father, the scary warrior, was kind. He cared about people and the good of the world. Rune reminded me of him. They both didn't speak much, but they would rip apart the world for those they loved. We listened to the birds chirp in their winter nests. A breeze blew by, and I pulled my jacket closer. I'd been in so many climates these past few weeks, my body didn't know what to feel.

"I'm glad you're here." I broke the silence. In the short time I'd spent with him, he'd been the best father for me. Verin's cold parenting pushed me to be quiet and be the perfect princess. Desmire wanted me to be me . . . to be happy with myself.

"I'm proud of who you've become. Your mother and I always knew you would be important to this world." The left side of his lips lifted and my eyes watered. I'd been a little teary-eyed lately. I could blame it on the pregnancy, but I've been very happy lately.

"Thanks." My full heart ached with love for him.

"Do you feel OK to train? I wanted to share some tricks with you." He stood and held out his hand. I felt pretty good today and hadn't used my magic much since I arrived home. It was there, though, tingling beneath the skin, waiting to be unleashed. I'd need to train soon and practice my new set of powers. I let him pull me up and waited to see what lessons he had planned. My father walked this planet for over nine hundred years, and I wanted to know everything he wanted to share with me. Some real father-daughter bonding. We walked down to the waterfall, a favorite setting in my family, far from people and possible casualties.

"Fire comes easy to you because of your personality. Control is a learned element. Fire is life; it's energy is an extension of yourself . . . the dragon who burns deep within."

Fire sparked from his hands, and I did the same. Its warm tendrils tickled my fingers. He was right. Fire did come easy for me, despite it being an absorbed power. He grinned at my display, then the fire in his hand grew longer. He gripped it tight and threw his hand out. The fire cracked in the air as he wielded it like a whip. I willed my fire to become a weapon. Nothing.

"You have to think of your powers as a part of you, not an outside source." He laughed and the fire in his hands shifted into a sword. He slashed the air around him, then threw it at the waterfall where it maintained shape until it disintegrated in the water.

Think of my powers as part of me, not an outside source. I could do that. My boots dug into the dirt, then I steadied my legs as I lunged forward with my right foot. My hand shot out, and I imagined the fire extending beyond my hand, giving me more reach. A fire spike shot from my fingers and embedded in a tree. Not exactly what I went for, but I'd take it. Small progress counted, and I celebrated the little victory. My father nodded, then showed me more about controlling fire.

When my well of flames dried up, we shifted into our dragon forms, then took to the skies. He taught me how to fly faster than I had before, truly a useful technique I wished I had known in the desert. As we flew over the Hallowstag Woods, up the mountains, and circled back around, he told me about dragon history. Dragons spoke telepathically, if desired, like he did with me. Real dragons existed once. His family was gifted with the essence after his father saved the life of the great Onyx dragon. The Onyx dragon was black as the night sky and the oldest of its kind. As a gift, my father was born with the powers of the legendary beast. Verin hunted them in hopes of destroying Desmire, and as far as my father knew, there were no more dragons in all the realm.

"I've tried for many years to call for dragons, and none have come. I fear we are the last of a dying breed." His snout pointed ahead to the clouds, but I knew he wasn't really seeing the view in front of him.

When I was human, I had experienced an extinction crisis inside me. Humans were a dying breed, too. Ever since I made it to the Fae realm, I'd almost forgotten about the human survivors . . . the ones who managed to avoid the Dramens' grasp. They were out there, but their numbers dwindled, even in the other continents. I had asked Aminthe about it one day and she said Dramens were over there, too. They didn't call themselves that, but the bad humans had enslaved most of the survivors. No Fae was permitted to cross realms.

Something had to be done.

"I'm getting tired. I think I'm going home for dinner and rest." My stomach growled and the sound echoed across the mountains. He shifted his snout toward me and nodded.

"Rest easy, daughter." He spoke in my head, and my heart warmed. I flew back to the palace and shifted in the gardens. I'd never forget days like today, spending real one-on-one time with my dad. My *real* dad. I learned, I grew as a person, and I couldn't wait to share these memories with my baby. He or she was going to have a grandpa who loved her dearly and gave her the time and devotion she would need— something I had lacked growing up. After grabbing a bite to eat, I saw Nyx and promised to come try on the dress she had made for me after my nap. As soon as I made it to the door, Rune scooped me into his arms and carried me to the bed.

"You're one terrifying dragon." He chuckled against my chest. The heat of his body soothed me. I snuggled into him as he laid me down on the bed, then crawled in beside me.

"I'm just gonna nap for a bit. You don't have to stay." Truthfully I wanted him to be with me. We'd been apart for too long. I craved him constantly.

"I know." He kissed my head and held me close while I fell asleep.

Chapter Twenty-Seven

Dris

"Tor will faint when he sees you in that dress." Sapphira touched the lacy fabric of Nyx's dress as it hung on the wardrobe. We'd gathered in her room to wake her up with a pampering morning. Sapphira carried a tray full of delicious breakfast plates, and I had a bag filled with goodies to give her a mini-spa treatment. I rubbed the bride's foot, using special acupuncture techniques I had read about last night.

"It's amazing to see my design come to life . . . and so quickly." Nyx groaned as I pushed right into the arch of her foot.

"I'm so happy for you." Sapphira sat beside Nyx and cupped her hand over our friend's hand. I knew what the gift was, but I still smiled when her hands opened up to show sapphire earrings resting in Nyx's palm.

"In the human world, brides were supposed to have something blue. I don't know why, but I wanted to give you them, anyway." Sapphira shrugged and tears fell onto her cheeks. She'd been quite emotional lately, but every time I saw her cry, it was from feeling happy, which I found completely acceptable.

"I missed this." I smiled, and the girls looked at me.

"Last time we hung out like this was back in Crystoria. While it wasn't that long ago, it feels like ages. We've all grown so much." I expanded on my words. "Tor had just kissed you then, and now you're getting married in a few hours!" I giggled and Nyx choked out a laugh.

"You admitted to being in a thing with Emrys, that you liked him, and well . . . I can tell by the way you guys look at each other things are going well."

I splashed her leg with the water beneath her foot, which only made her laugh harder. Sapphira grinned but neither Nyx or I were gonna leave her out of this.

"You and Rune had finally mated. Now you're having a baby!"

Nyx nudged her and I resumed my friendly duty of spa day. Sapphira placed her hand on her stomach that had grown in the past few days.

"It's beautiful to see how much has changed. Everyone is happy right now." I spoke wistfully. It was hard to describe, even for a walking dictionary like me. Our smiles dimmed slightly.

"It's moments like this that we must celebrate living in. We know what's coming and you can be damn sure I will fight for times like this. I love you girls." Sapphira placed a hand on both of our shoulders and I still had no words. No matter what horrors came our way, we had these memories and friends to keep us fighting.

"It's gonna be fun to have a little baby around the palace." Nyx broke the short silence that had settled over our thoughts.

"How's Rune doing with thoughts of being a dad?" I asked. I watched her play with the tiger's eye ring on her finger. I suspected we'd have another wedding to plan soon. Neither of them seemed to be in a rush, but Rune wasn't exactly a patient male.

"He is already wrapped around the baby's finger. I couldn't imagine parenting without him, especially with this baby's big destiny." She sighed, and we understood her heavy heart. They are the best parents for that child. I was shocked at first to hear about the choice they made at the dying Heart Tree. Save humanity and release magic, but at a price. I'd suspected the cruel fate of my aunt Celestine, but still cried when Sapphira told me she truly died.

"I can't imagine anyone else being more perfect to handle a powerful baby than you two. Rune would go werewolf on someone and rip their heads apart after you used your plethora of magic on them first. It's gonna be great, and I can't wait to squish those chubby cheeks." Nyx pinched invisible cheeks by Sapphira's stomach. I snorted, but wholeheartedly agreed. Rune and Sapphira both had zero remorse when it came to battle. I think fighting counted as foreplay in their relationship.

"It's true," I confirmed, and switched to the other foot. Sapphira rubbed Nyx's shoulders as best as she knew how, and I painted her nails lavender as she requested. The rest of the morning went by so quickly. We laughed, cried, and felt beyond happy to be with friends again. Emrys brought us lunch without seeing the bride. I worked on her hair while Sapphira ate fruit and watched. She knew she would be no help in that department. While Nyx loved the girl, she did not want the princess touching her beautiful lavender tresses.

"I'm here for emotional support and the snacks," Sappphira teased. I'd been instructed to do her makeup last. Princess orders. A knock startled us and I stepped toward the door but Sapphira beat me to it.

"I have one last gift for you," she sang, and Nyx watched her curiously. Interested, I didn't know what the surprise was either. Sapphira opened the door all the way, and four women squealed as they strode into the room, each with pastel-colored hair and luxurious dresses. I guessed who they were seconds before Nyx burst into tears. Sapphira somehow had brought Nyx's family to Crysia to see her get married. They hugged her tightly. At least twenty years had passed since they had been together. Communications had been cut off with Verin in charge, and I hadn't heard if her family survived. I quietly strode to Sapphira and watched as the sisters basked in their happy reunion.

"Rika?" I had to know, and Sapphira nodded. The queen's elusive advisor had been so busy lately, I hadn't seen her.

"You guys are my family. I'd do anything to make you happy." She pulled me in for a hug before two of the sisters grabbed our hands and lightly pulled us into the giant group hug.

I'd do whatever necessary to keep my "family" safe. I'd use every book in my library and every word to my advantage. I wouldn't let Verin take them from me.

The girls helped Nyx get ready as Sapphira and I left to get dressed ourselves. With the Princess's new locs, she didn't need anything to make her hair look gorgeous. She glowed perfectly with her pregnancy hormones. I, however, wore a bold choice of dress to surely cause my mate to fight from keeping his hands off of me.

Chapter Twenty-Eight

Rune

I admit to being a poor brother to Tor. I had pushed him away and ignored him like I did everyone else. It was easier. But we'd changed over our journey to Crystoria from rivals to family. He left his mate to help me find Sapphira. In all his young years, he had refused to treat me differently. So when he requested I stand beside him as he married his mate, I agreed without hesitation. Times changed, and while I couldn't promise I'd be the perfect brother, mate, general, or father, I'd try to be. There's nothing in this world I wouldn't do for them, including trying to be the best version of myself. His light blue hair looked like burning flames on his head. The whole family looked like a painter's palette. I know if Sapphira walked toward me, I'd fight collapsing to my knees before her. So while everyone watched Nyx walk toward Tor in her skintight lacy dress, I shifted to look at Tor. He smiled bigger than I'd ever seen. Tears lined his eyes; his hands flexed at his sides. I pulled at the embroidered tunic against my neck to let the air cool the emotions heating my insides. While I was the older brother, Tor had taught me more about family and allowing myself to be vulnerable. I loved the jerk, and experiencing this new stage of his life was a gift.

Sapphira wiped her tears on a small cloth on the other side of Tor. She and Dris stood on the bride's side of the garden in matching lavender satin dresses. My mate cried as her oldest friend reached Tor and grasped his hand. Their vows passed quickly as the queen wrapped their joined hands in a shimmering ribbon. They each drank from the blessed water in a diamond goblet, to give the couple blessings from our purest essence. The water had once flowed from the Heart Tree. They kissed to seal the marriage, and Emrys hollered his excitement, which erupted in the rest of the crowd. Hoots and congratulatory screams filled the air. I didn't even fight the smile on my face as my brother turned to me, full of love and pure happiness.

"Congratulations, brother." I placed my hand on his shoulder and he nodded. He then scooped up his bride and kissed her while spinning in a circle. He carried her down the aisle and everyone else headed to the throne room. The newlyweds would have a moment to themselves to digest what had happened before spending the rest of the night dancing and laughing with their loved ones.

"That was beautiful." My mate slid to my side and I wrapped my arms around her. We watched every rejoice and cheer in the palace.

"I'm happy for him."

"Me, too. He deserved someone amazing and I can't think of anyone else who fits the part. Luckily destiny agreed by choosing them as mates." She kissed my arm, and I reciprocated on top of her head.

"Destiny doesn't make mistakes. She gave me you, my pain-in-the-ass, bath-obsessed, fierce warrior who drools on me when she sleeps." I smiled as her body shook from her laughter. I lived for her joy.

"We should probably head inside soon." She patted my arm and tried to untangle herself from me, only I didn't let her go.

"Probably." I brushed the spot behind her ear with my lips. Goosebumps rose over her skin, and I soothed them with a kiss. Her fingers gripped my arms, and I smirked.

"Sapphira! Nyx . . . oops." Dris ran into the garden, then stopped herself when she saw us having a moment. Sapphira snapped out of her lusty haze, and I let her go.

"I'm coming." My mate ensured she swayed her ass a little dramatically as she walked away. I shook my head; the woman drove me insane.

"Runeeeeee," the wind called my name, and I closed my eyes. Ever since magic had been released, my connection to nature had intensified. I followed the whispers to Celestine's cave. I heard the music from the throne room and wanted to return to the party.

"Runnneee." It beckoned me, and I marched through the rock cave to see a fire lit with tea sitting on the grass.

"Celestine," I grumbled, and sat on the grass ready for whatever she had to tell me. I trusted the spirit now, but that didn't mean I liked everything she had to say. Her pets rubbed against me, and I nudged them away. I wasn't a big fan of domesticated pets. Lucky was different, even though I refused to admit it to anyone.

"Prince Rune, it's good to see you." She watched me with her big owl eyes. I watched her patiently waiting for her to get to the point. Celestine only showed up when something important needed to be said. Her surprise visit had meaning, and she only wanted me to hear it.

"Very well. Verin is after your child. He knows about the Heart Tree's essence within your babe. This war will no longer be about covering the earth under his dark reign but changing the will of magic itself. If he raises your child as his own, he will use those precious gifts to give life and bless the earth with vile and evil magic. No one will be able to stop him, then."

All thought froze in my head. I couldn't breathe, couldn't move, as fear struck me in the chest. "He won't touch our child," I growled, rage seeping into my vision.

"I see all futures dear and I am telling you because there is a possibility that you must prevent."

161

She floated closer, and a snarled warning burst from my lungs. Spirit or no, she should not come closer right now.

"When the war comes, two men dressed in red will emerge from the blood-soaked earth. Kill them, and save your child. I do not part with this information lightly, but there must be no mistakes. Kill the red warriors, and save your mate and your child." Pressure on my shoulder from her touch took away the blinding rage that distracted me from soaking in her words.

"They will die." I remembered the vow to my mate that we'd take on the world together. This knowledge would infuriate her; destroy the little bit of happiness she had.

"Sapphira?" The seer knew why I spoke my mate's name, and nodded knowingly.

"She suspects but does not need to know. Doing so will make her reckless, and she will need a clear head for what's to come."

I swallowed the lump in my throat. I never lied or kept something like this from my mate. It would not be an easy feat, but I had to do it. The seer was right. Sapphira would obsess and seek out a way to prevent anything from happening and drive herself to insanity. I nearly lost her when she took out her core and became human for twenty years.

"Enjoy the time given, and bask in your mate's glow. There is no preventing Verin's war now. Be happy until it arrives." She smiled at me, then winked. Her body vanished and I glared at the tea without really seeing it.

"Fuck!" I roared, my hands running down my face. I downed the tea in a matter of seconds, and a warm sensation chased the lingering anger out of my system. Celestine, the meddlesome seer, was right again. War would descend upon us, but we had to make the most of the life we had now.

I dashed out of the cave and strode into the party with a neutral face. No one would know the secrets I harbored, and I wouldn't tell them. Tor and Nyx danced with contented smiles. His hands grabbed her ass when he pulled her close and thought no one watched. Dris and Emrys talked with the bride's family. They laughed and Dris nodded vigorously, finding the conversation riveting. I pushed thoughts of the red warriors into the back of my mind. Sapphira's laugh caught my attention and I moved for her. My fire and my balm, she greeted me with a kiss, then pulled me to the dance floor.

Chapter Twenty-Nine

Sapphira

Rune's hand stayed pressed to my stomach all night long. He refused to miss any more of my pregnancy. He stayed by my side through every talk with the healer, Rista, and patiently waited to feel movement. He loved me and this baby more than anything in the world. He'd spend as much time with me as he could while acting out his general duties. Tor and Nyx had gone to the edges of the kingdom for a mini-honeymoon while we waited for our allies to arrive. It'd been a week since the wedding. In the downtime, I either trained with Rune or my father, relaxed with Dris and Emrys, or had tea with my mom.

Suddenly, the baby moved and Rune's hand flexed. Whether he knew I was awake or not, his body scooted closer, and his hand splayed across my skin. I bit back my smile and hoped the child moved again. The request was granted, and the baby decided to get a head start on warrior training. Rune inhaled sharply, and I placed my hand over his.

"So strong," he breathed. The words tickled the hairs on my neck.

"Just like his or her daddy," I gleamed and felt my mate smile behind me.

"Just like us both."

"Yeah, the baby is doomed. A pain-in-the-ass mom and a grumpy dad. Poor thing." The child bumped hard beneath our hands.

"Have you thought of names?" Rune's question surprised me. I honestly, couldn't say I had. Which made me feel slightly guilty. That was something mother's do when waiting for their child to arrive. Pick names, decorate a nursey. From the moment I found out about the child, I'd been in battle, and a fight to survive. I'd only been home a few days and there had been so many emotions with added excitement to occupy my thoughts. I shook my head and asked him the same question.

"Phoenix for a boy, it means dark red like a ruby, and the bird was known to be kind yet fierce." I turned around to face him as he spoke. His hand went back to my stomach to wait for more movement.

"And for a girl?" I grinned, loving this conversation with him. He paused to think for a moment then kissed my lips gently.

"Ildri, it means fire and peace. Our child needs to be both." I loved that he thought about this and told him so.

"Sometimes the separation was too great. Thinking about our life with the child kept me sane." Tears welled in my eyes from his admission. I wished I could take that pain away from him.

"I am fine, Sapphira." His thumb lifted to wipe the tears away . . . such a soft touch for my badass warrior.

"I know, we should focus on today and what's to come. Like where we will live with the baby. Here? Take over another room? My mother's room had a spot for a nursery. She turned it into a meditation space after I grew out of it. We could live somewhere else in the kingdom." The words poured from my lips and Rune smiled with each rambled word.

"I do not care as long as the babe sleeps in a cradle when it's not necessary to be snuggled. I need alone time with you in the bed for sinful reasons." My body heated.

"You would say that." I reached to caress his bare chest. I'd yet to tire of the sight of him, all his muscles, the body created from battle, with those icy eyes and dark ebony hair. The most gorgeous man I'd ever seen.

"Whatever you want, it's yours. If you want a place separate from the palace, I will build us a home with my bare hands."

"There's that sweetness again, spoiling me rotten."

"I vowed to be sweet to you every day for the rest of our immortal lives." He smiled, and I pushed his chest to climb on top of him. His breathtaking smile lit up the room.

166

"That you did. I warned you I'd become obsessed with hearing your words." My head dropped close to his lips.

"Shall I give you more sweetness, my princess?" He rolled his hips upward, and I shivered at the contact between my legs.

"Give me all the precious words, my prince." I challenged him for the fun of it. Rune and I lived for that fire between us. We would never be an ordinary couple, and I valued that. He hummed beneath me while I circled my hips over his length. He accepted my challenge as I guided him inside me. I rode my prince, while he fed me beautiful compliments and dreams he'd whispered long ago. When the need to conquer drove him to the brink, he lifted me off him and spun me around on all fours. He plunged into me and relentlessly drove us both over the edge. We collapsed onto the sheets, and my mate rested his head against my stomach.

"In my youth, I never wanted a mate. They'd just be another person to hate me, to fear me. Then you showed up. Spitfire of a woman, who did not fear me but challenged me. My heart became yours that day in the Hallowstags. When I thought you were trapped in the onyx, my love never wavered until that day you came back into my life as a human. I vowed then that no matter what happened I wouldn't let you go." He kissed where our child moved against him.

"My mind believed I loved another, but my beast, my heart knew you. It knew the mischievous look in your eyes, the fire beneath that smile, and the unyielding love in your chest that called out for me. We are endless. No matter how long we walk this earth, our love will transcend time and space. When the world takes it lasts breath, what we share will live amongst the stars. But for now, I will not live another moment without calling you mine in every way I can." His gaze met mine, and I saw the undiluted love shine brightly at me.

"Marry me, Sapphira. You're already my moon and my mate. Now be my wife." He smiled, so full of hope and love. How could I deny this male anything?

"Now those were some beautiful words, mate." I sat up, and he mirrored me. Our faces were a headspace away. My hands cradled his jaw, as I stared into those icy depths.

"You are my solid ground for when I feel unstable. You are the war. You are the warrior who fought for me against all odds. You are my hope in a world of fear. I love you, Rune, and I am honored to marry you . . . to be your wife, fight by your side, and give you lots of beautiful babies." I added the last part knowing Rune loved me being pregnant. He would be a very happy father to be blessed with more than one. His lips lunged for mine and I cried against his kiss. We were endless, and that was more than enough for me.

"I love you." He kissed me with every ounce of his essence.

"I love you, you sweet and growling jackass."

We kissed for hours until it was time to meet with the others for dinner. Only we ended up with more guests than I thought for the meal. Some of our allies had arrived early.

Chapter Thirty

Sapphira

"Soon," my mate whispered and I stared at the growing allies before me. We'd tried multiple times over the past three days to sneak off and get married, only to be pulled in various directions. We barely had time to say "I love you" before crashing in bed. Kunsula and Kuanish, the twins from Asil Tas, had arrived. Dris and Kunsula instantly connected over their bookworm tendencies. They'd brought around two thousand of their soldiers, who were some of the greatest archers in the world. My mother and Rune had organized setting up camps for all the soldiers in a large field next to a rushing river. Then the Ice Queen arrived with her elite guards, as well as fifteen hundred soldiers. Both kingdoms left behind some warriors to protect their people as they should, but it was an amazing sight to see they had brought that many. The variety of armor colors looked beautiful. The Lunnayian's white armor appeared blindingly bright beside the Asil Tas's orange and blue cloth and leather suits. My mother requested my presence in every meeting of the leaders, and I trained when I wasn't resting my pregnant feet. So to say my life was hectic would be an understatement.

Luckily my friends helped to take a load off my shoulders when they could. Dris kept Kunsula busy in the library and gardens, while Tor practiced archery with Kuanish, who eagerly taught the prince what he knew. The Ice Queen and my mother got along quite nicely, and I wondered what trouble they would get into once my aunt from Crystoria arrived. My aunt had sent word of their departure a few days ago and would get here any day.

With every passing moment, Crysia became a more powerful and hope-driven opponent. Verin's army would surely pause at the sight before them. Each of the leaders touched hands with me so I'd absorb a little of their powers. Nyx asked if it made them feel vulnerable giving it away, and the Ice Queen's reply surprised me.

"We are here because Verin threatens the whole world. It would be selfish to withhold power that could make the difference. We sacrifice a particle of our essence so that she may have every tool available to defeat him. Vulnerability is not weakness. You become weak when you allow your vulnerabilities to define you."

Being in that woman's presence made me feel like a badass.

Her guards trained with Najen and Rune, which I found comical because the women clearly had an edge that even Rune had difficulties deflecting. I aimed to learn every technique and strategy I could in the waking hours. The peaceful, joyous days of having picnics in the garden were over. I held these dear, short-lived times close to me in moments where my body ached from so much training. Being pregnant didn't make fighting any easier. No one refused to take it easy on me with my diamond skin power activated, but carrying around the extra weight made me short of breath quicker than normal. My breasts and stomach kept expanding, and I expected to topple over.

"You're really fine-tuning your powers. Just think, not too long ago you were setting your curtains on fire, now you can wield fire, ice, earth, and light to your will, oh Warrior Princess." Nyx held a glass of water in her outstretched hand for me. I guzzled the liquid and looked at the warriors training in the courtyard.

"It's beautiful to see so many people come together like this." She sat beside me and I rested my head against her shoulder. It was inspiring to see Fae from different kingdoms ally to fight alongside each other.

Tor's messy hair came into view, his head shifting from side to side like he searched for someone in particular. His gaze landed on me and he rushed over. He rubbed the back of his neck and glanced at the palace. Instantly, fear gripped at my chest.

"What is it?"

He swallowed thickly. "My parents have arrived."

I winced at his words.

"Shit, where's Rune?" I searched for my mate, but he wasn't training in the courtyard. He didn't need to face his father alone. I would be there.

"He's in the palace somewhere. I couldn't find him." Tor grimaced and I raced inside. I heard loud voices before I turned the corner to the throne room.

"General Rune, put him down before he pisses on the floor." My father's voice echoed throughout the room from where he stood on the dais. Mother sat on her throne, lips a straight line while her eyes lit up with hidden laughter. Ten men stood with their swords pointed at my mate. His hand gripped his father's throat, as he held the man's body two inches off the ground. Rune's mother stood to the side, her hand at her mouth but she did not rush to aid her husband.

"Rune, we need him." I walked to my mate and placed a hand on his shoulder. A muscle in his jaw ticked, but he slowly released his father with a hateful glare in his eye.

"Control that feral beast before I take my army home." He spoke to my mother and everyone in the room stilled. Rune's lip curled, and I thought for a second his werewolf would come out, teeth snapping. The full moon was tonight, so his savage side tended to be more prevalent during this time. Before I could say something, my mother stood gracefully, then descended the dais.

"While I appreciate your support to win against Verin, I will not allow you to dishonor my daughter, my home, and my general." She leaned in and said something in his ear. His face became pale. Whatever threat my mother gave him, it scared him. Rune grabbed my hand and pulled me off to the side of the room. His arms wrapped around me in a hug, and I knew he needed me. Dealing with his father had the potential to set off hundreds of traumatic memories in his mind.

He was hurting.

"I love you, my sexy mate who rubs my feet after a long day. The beautiful male whose sweet words and growls bring this princess to her knees. My mate, my match, my strength, and my passion." I rubbed my fingers over his scalp, soothing the hurt. I pushed a tinge of Nyx's calming magic into him. A shiver shook his strong body. My mother had Rika escort the King and Queen of Regno Dei Lupi to their suites in the palace. Najen would show the guards where to sleep and the soldier camps.

"He walked in like he owned the place and asked where's the bitch princess that demanded he come. I lost it. I can handle his cruel words against me, but I will not tolerate words about my mate. My home," he growled. His hands cupped my cheeks to kiss me.

"It's going to be OK. Whatever mother threatened him with seemed to scare him. I don't think we will have issues going forward." I kissed him once more before stepping back.

"She threatened to have him put down like a broken wolf and seat his firstborn on the throne. She is more powerful than him, and he knows it. Having me take his place is his worst nightmare." Rune smirked, his eyes lifted, and I saw my mom wink out of the corner of my eye. Not everyone wanted to be like their parents when they grew up. Rune's father was a perfect case of that. But I wanted to be a badass like my mom.

"Well that was a great family reunion." Tor slid up to our side, Nyx on his arm.

"Wait until he finds out you're married," Rune huffed and Tor grinned. Fighting and family reunions . . . what else is war good for but bringing everyone together, whether you like them or not.

Chapter Thirty -One
Emrys

Nothing happens around the palace without me hearing about it. So as Sapphira's best friend and loyal blood-bound spider, I declared Crysia in a state of emergency. Rune and Sapphira had been trying to sneak off and get married but their lives had gotten too busy. Daddy Wolfstrom made Rune's attitude mega sour, and Tor hasn't been any better. In fact, during last night's full moon, Sapphira kept Rune busy in the Hallowstags so he wouldn't run back to the palace and eat his father.

Unbeknownst to my friends, I plotted and planned the best wedding Sapphira could want. Being the commander of the operations, I used my powers to eavesdrop on conversations to determine the best time to make it happen. Since every commander needs soldiers, I appointed Nyx to be on outfit duty. Dris would gather the people Sapphira would want to witness. Then Tor and I had to get Rune to the waterfall for the the magical union. He was a little extra grumpy and tired from the shift, but I had no doubt we could make it work. I looked at the sun's position and reckoned the time had come. If my little soldiers had done their jobs, Sapphira and the guests should be at the waterfall. I noticed Tor tried to get the werewolf's attention, but the man kept walking to the courtyard. I'd probably get my ass beat later for the plan that shot through my mind, but it would be worth it.

"Rune! Sapphira! By the waterfall!" I yelled in a panic and the male's face turned menacing. Yep, I was so dead. He raced to the waterfall, then stopped dead in his tracks. Tor and I caught up seconds later and I grinned. I had pulled it off. In the clearing near the falls stood the queen with Sapphira dressed in a satin white gown. Her hair had flowers weaved into her locs, and she smiled brightly at the sight of her mate. Dris had kept the gathering small because she knew both Princess and Prince didn't want a big extravagant wedding. The rulers of the other kingdoms she'd met on her passage home stood on each side of the makeshift aisle of flower petals. The male with fish scales on his face nodded at me. Rune's mother stood next to Najen and his husband. The king had apparently opted out of the wedding, and I doubted anyone missed him.

Rune grumbled beside me and shrugged. "I planned a surprise wedding. You can thank me later." I patted him on the shoulder and Tor burst into laughter.

"Come, dearest general. The time has come." Queen Olyndria waved us over. I shuffled up to my spot in the crowd next to my sexy librarian. Tor kissed Nyx on the cheek as they stood on the other side of us. Daddy Desmire hugged his daughter once, then winked at Rune and took his place to the side of Sapphira.

"I'm just as surprised as you are," she whispered to her mate, as he clasped their hands together.

"You're beautiful," he breathed as the queen started her spiel. They stared into each other's eyes as they promised eternity as husband and wife. They drank from the diamond goblet and smiled through their first kiss as a married couple. I'd heard the stories; I knew they'd been waiting for more than twenty years to reach this moment. I'm glad I was able to make it happen.

"All hail, Sapphira and Rune Wolfstrom!" someone hollered from the crowd, and I joined in.

"This was a fabulous idea." Dris hugged me and I kissed her head. It really was. Everything had come together beautifully. We had nearly nine thousand soldiers ready for war. The princess and Rune were getting their happy ending. All we needed to do was beat Verin and live happily ever after.

"I'm so proud of you, Rune. You and Tor have become men of honor. I hope you will allow me to visit and play with my grandchild in the future." Rune's mom hugged her two sons, then wrapped her slender arms around Sapphira. The werewolf didn't snarl at her, but he didn't exactly seem joyous, either. His wife picked up on that and spoke for him.

"You're welcome to Crysia anytime." Her mate's fingers tightened around her waist.

"Emrys," Rune called into the crowd until I stepped forward.

"Whatever party you planned, cancel it. We're celebrating in other ways." Rune scooped his wife into his arms. Blush coated her cheeks but she didn't contradict his command. They said goodbye to everyone before Rune took off with his bride in his arms.

"Party food in the throne room for anyone who's interested," I announced to the crowd and most everyone walked toward the tall wooden doors of the palace.

"Kunsula, walk with us!" Dris wrapped her right arm around mine and her left around her new friend.

"That was a beautiful wedding. In our kingdom, the marriage ceremonies are performed over the course of a week. We have multiple feasts in the couple's honor. There is a blessings dance the family does around them. Then they say their vows to each other and blow the light out on a white candle together as a married couple." The woman's hearty laugh caught the attention of everyone around us. She didn't notice and kept talking. Dris had been enamored by her tales of the faraway kingdom, and I loved watching her passions be fed.

179

"In Lunnaya Skala, we only marry on the full moon. Waters from the great glacier are collected. We believe it blesses the couple with light and fullness in their marriage. Once you drink it, you kiss, and then you are married. We keep it simple." The Ice Queen entered the conversation. I had to say I liked their way of doing things . . . simple and to the point.

"We'll have to visit sometime. You know, once we survive everything," Dris commented and I gripped her arm tighter. Verin had yet to show his true hand, and the waiting was starting to get to people.

"Yes, I will throw a party in your honor. You will love our famous baursak. Delicious friend dough with powdered sugar," Kunsula gushed and her brother groaned behind us.

"Now I'm craving them."

"We have some sweets inside. Hopefully that'll take the edge off." I gave the guy some hope and he moaned a thank you. His steps picked up the pace to get to the sweets before the rest of us.

"Getting Sapphira ready for the wedding without telling her what was planned was hard. I think it turned out great, though. She looked really happy." Nyx's voice came from behind us next to Kuanish and Tor. Dris nodded while Kunsula gushed about the princess's dress and hair. We hung out in the throne room, gobbled up the decadent pastries, and exchanged stories about all the kingdoms. Dris's eyes grew wide with every passing tale. I knew she loved

Crysia and the library here. However, I could see her interest in exploring the world. I wanted her to see and experience everything life had to offer us.

"Your majesty! Queen Olyndria!" A guard frantically burst into the room, scanning for the queen.

"Report," she demanded, and a dark feeling settled over my body.

"Allies from Crystoria just arrived."

The Crystorians' arrival wasn't exactly panic-worthy. We knew they would come to aid us in the upcoming fight. No sooner did my thought occur, then Queen Denisiri walked through the door in her full battle armor of gold, hair aflame.

"Our scouts reported my brother's army is about a day behind our arrival. War has almost reached Crysia's borders." The fire beneath her tattoos rolled, and the darkness around me settled in my gut. The good times, and joyous bonding was over.

The time for battle had arrived.

Chapter Thirty-Two

Sapphira

We all knew the happy moments would end. But knowing didn't stop the hearts around me from deflating. War was inevitable. Crysia had gathered an army to shake the realm, and it still wasn't enough. Dris led a team of flying Fae to scout the soldiers Verin had summoned. Monsters that haven't been seen in centuries stomped alongside Dramens and evil Fae from the badlands. We were outnumbered and I feared outmatched. Giant snakes slithered down the mountains, and creatures with three horns that stood taller than an elephant moved through the forests. We'd decided the best place to fight would be three miles north of Crysia between the great mountains. There were trees for cover, a large open meadow, and a river that meandered into the Hallowstags. Even Verin wouldn't take his army into those woods.

The best chance we had was to bottleneck the soldiers between the mountains instead of risking them surrounding us. Crysia's city and palace would be guarded by soldiers of all the kingdoms. The diamond wall would hopefully protect our home. The people had been evacuated inside the shelter. Rune spent time showing the guards who'd stay behind the secret passages he had created to the other side of the mountain, if the people need to flee. I didn't like the thought, but we had to be prepared.

A furry head bumped against me and I smiled. My fingers scratched at Cara's head, and I was grateful she had survived the last battle. Rune mentioned the harem in Verin's palace and that our beloved pets took the women to their homes. Cara returned this morning with a passenger. One of Verin's mistresses wanted to fight; her electric powers would give us an edge.

"They're approaching!" Dris yelled as soon as she shifted from her second flight over the army. Her thin diamond armor shimmered in the afternoon's light.

"Archers!" Kuanish commanded his people and blue bows lifted into position.

Foot soldiers stood behind those with riding creatures. Those who shifted into animals were already in the form that suited battle most. The air felt stagnant, like it was fearful to rattle the beasts headed our way. Queens and kings watched as my father swooped into the clearing before us. The ground shook as he landed. His massive head lifted and a vicious roar unlike anything I'd heard before released a shock wave that rattled the mountains. Our soldiers staggered a bit to find their stances again.

"He calls for aid." Rune stood beside me, his eyes wide at my father.

"Aid?" I looked around at all the aid we could muster.

Rune shook his head. "There are other inhabitants of this realm, legendary creatures that do not pick sides in Fae battles. His roar was a command and plea."

My hand grasped my mates. I needed his strength to keep me steady. Aid would be great, but I didn't know what creatures he spoke of. So unless monsters like that demon in the ice mountain had friends who would fight on our side, I couldn't devote much thought to my father's plea.

"They're here," my mother announced, as the first wave of soldiers broke through the trees on the other side of the meadow. Verin and his daughter, Lethirya, rode their large reptiles. The massive snakes slithered at their sides. I detected the king and queen of the Dramens as they stopped their black and brown horses just behind Verin. It was an army created to eviscerate all in its path.

"We cannot win," Rune's father muttered, and I knew I should have let Rune eat him last night.

"Courage husband." His wife withdrew a black sword from her side, eyes on the encroaching enemy, a fierce grandmother ready to fight and protect the future of her grandbaby. The soldiers behind us whispered, and fear weaved through the variety of colored armor and weapons. My aunt placed a hand on my mother, and she moved her creature forward

184

with a heavy breath. The mad queen, who was mad no more, stood strong in front of our quivering forces on top a white Pegasus. I watched, enamored, as she lifted her dual-bladed staff in the air, gathering the attention of everyone.

"Your blood races at the sight before you now. The fear of a hopeless battle grips at the beating heart inside your chest. Every soldier beside you shares your fears, your hopes for victory, and your courage. Across this field, an army has gathered to wipe the light from our world. They are fighting against life, joy, and love. That is their weakness. You cannot win when fighting against the greatest powers in our hearts. We, the children of magic, of this realm, fight for our friends, our family, and for each other. It is that strength of having something to fight for that they cannot defeat. Today, darkness will not wrap its evil claws around our light." Her voice grew as she paced her white Pegasus across the line of our allies. Her words straightened the spines of everyone who listened.

"We fight to save our world! We fight against tyranny! We fight for love and freedom!" Her belted words soaked into the soldier's chests. Weapons lifted to the sky. Cheers and guttural chants grew among the masses.

"We fight for our lives; we fight for victory!" The sun's rays shot through my mother's diamond-spiked crown, and tiny rainbows danced across our armor. She turned her Pegasus to face the enemy. Our army quivered no longer.

"SQUAAAA!" A screech echoed between the mountains.

"Luna," the Ice Queen called to the air, and a dot in the sky grew larger as it neared. Blue and white flames took shape in the form of a three-foot bird with wings sparkling with icy feathers and a white body that looked like fresh snow. Ice and fire swirled in its wake as it landed on the outstretched arm of its queen.

"That's an ice phoenix." Voices whispered behind us, and I felt the strength of every heart turn solid in their courage. We would fight, and we would crush the darkness back into the depths of hell from where it slithered from.

"For our child, for our endless love." I looked to my mate and he kissed me with abandon. Silvio grumbled beneath him.

"I'll always find my way to you," he promised, and I repeated the words to him.

"We'll meet for celebratory ice cream later." Nyx placed a hand on my shoulder. Her purple hair was tied back into a bun, and the diamond armor radiated an ethereal appeal instead of a soldier.

"I'll take ice cream and a bottle of wine," Dris added, touching Nyx's shoulder. Tor and Emrys nodded, weapons in their hands. My friends, through countless struggles, fought at my side, and somewhere along the way we became a family. I glanced at our new allies. Friends I may have known for a short time but they still felt like part of my family. These people were here to give their lives for hope, for the world we want to live in. A better world, a free world.

"To victory!" I screamed. Hope burned in my heart, hot as a flame and sturdy as the earth. My family both old and new roared at my side while my father released his fire on the enemy's line. The great battle against an age of darkness had begun.

Chapter Thirty-Three

Sapphira

Fire collided with sand walls. Teeth and claws scraped against armor. The sounds of war rippled across the realm. Verin and the leaders of the Dramens remained still as their armies rushed for us head on. The bottlenecking idea worked but where one soldier fell, two more leaped over the dead body. My father flew over the hordes of monsters, spraying fire for miles. Yet they pushed onward. Rune ripped the earth apart, and the massive snakes fell to their deaths. The elephant-like creatures tripped and stumbled as the ground shook. A small victory but the war was far from over. Arrows flew into the sky at rapid speed, Fae in red and black fell to the ground.

I lifted my hand and threw my hatchet at the Dramen who barreled toward me. Cara jumped at the male behind him, and I leaned down to snatch my weapon back. My eyes scanned the clashing warriors for my mate and my friends. Dris was ten yards away, flying on her wolfhawk with a bow firing arrows into the enemies' forces. Silvio's blast from his swirling chest of powers reverberated across the meadow, deep in Verin's rushing territory. I couldn't see Nyx or Tor or Emrys, but I knew they were alive. I'd feel it if they died; a part of them lived in me and always would. Cara swatted great beasts, and I slammed a blade into their disoriented skulls. We had a system that worked, until a large red tail smacked into my chest, knocking me off Cara. Again, I thanked the diamond skin for saving me from true harm. I'd worn extra armor for protection when the power wore off, but I hoped it would last until I no longer had need of it.

"Time to see who is better, cousin." The eerie voice of my nightmares, Lethirya, broke through my muddled thoughts. She wore her father's signature colors; her black hair rested against her armor in a long braid. She jumped off her lizard, and we circled each other. The soldiers around gave us a wide berth, knowing not to interfere with their princess of darkness and her prey. However, I was no sheep to slaughter. I was a fucking dragon, and this bitch was already scorched. She only needed to realize it.

Cara snuck to the side while Lethirya stared me down, her smile lifted toward the edge of her pointed eyes. My beast snarled as she lunged for the neck of my cousin's red lizard. They rolled across the grass, snapping and bodies crashing in a battle for the death. I took advantage of the surprise and hooked my axe into my holster, then unsheathed my sword. Every ounce of me screamed to unleash my powers, to raze the evil before me. But I could handle this female without them for now.

"Let's do this." She laughed maniacally and pushed off the ground with her legs to lunge for me.

Her sword was raised high, and I struck low. Metal scraped against metal, and her growl rolled over my senses. I dropped my center of gravity and kicked at her knees. She leaped to the side and rolled. Every move Najenand Rune taught me came to play in our dual. Instinctually, I punched with my bare hand to hit her face. The impact would not only cause damage but also absorb some of her power. My opponent sensed the motivations behind my attacks and avoided them. She would not give me an extra edge in this battle.

"Sneaky little cousin. To think you could steal from me. You are inferior, too weak to handle a power such as mine. That's why I was gifted with it, instead of you. What good is a sprinkle of borrowed magic if you can never wield it at its highest potential?" She shrieked, her blade coming down hard against mine. Over and over she sliced at me, hoping to land a blow. My knees buckled the slightest and she smiled.

Oh no, bitch. My foot slammed into the ground. Fire tickled my tongue as I grew hotter and hotter within. Suddenly, when smoke fled my nostrils, I opened my mouth and a great roar of fire blasted three feet from my lips. My cousin's eyes widened as she took in the beast I could become. My fire-breathing stunt made her take several steps back. I lifted my hands and quickly flung ice stakes at her. She dodged them by mere seconds but they collided with another enemy who wasn't as quick. One after another I threw the ice spikes at her. She rolled and leaped away with heavy pants. Her hand reached out and a portal grew large enough for her to jump through. Coward.

Cara's growl captured my attention, and I darted to my beast. My sword sliced every enemy in sight. Blood soaked her mouth and long neck. I sobbed, fearing her death a second time. But upon inspection, I saw she had been bitten twice on the back, and blood came from the dead lizard on the ground. She had bested the beast. Her head lowered for me to climb onto her, but I refused. She didn't need my body wiggling over her wounds.

"Keep kicking ass, Cara. I love you." I brushed my head against hers once. She purred, then we parted. Her sand-colored body jumped into a group of soldiers, their screams cut off by the sound of breaking bones and ripping flesh.

"Die!" A Dramen with black feathers attacked with a large axe and I jumped to the side just before the blade collided with my head. My body whirled around, sword gripped tight in my hands to see an arrow sticking out of his head.

"Nice to see your footwork has improved." Tor's teasing voice came from my right and I winked at him. Always the protector, no matter what he was to me, he would remain my knight in shining armor.

"Where's Nyx?" I grunted, as a gorilla beast with extra arms tried to crush me with huge pounding fists. I stomped the ground twice and willed the dirt to become like quicksand. The beast hollered as each inch of its body sank into the earth. Tor had shot two more soldiers in the head before he answered me.

"She is about fifteen yards behind us, using that new move I taught her with the dual swords. For a proper princess, she's really learned how to get her hands dirty." He grinned as his mate whirled around. Two blades spun with each step. She was something else, and I loved watching her kick ass.

A loud roar vibrated the ground, and Tor cautiously glanced behind me. My feet shifted and I saw what had him anxious. The sun descended its last strip of light below the horizon. Night had reached our battle. In the distance, a werewolf howled for blood and his mate.

Chapter Thirty-Four

Rune's Werewolf Side

Bullets and swords tried to take my beast down, but none could stop me. My body rejected both; their metal shells riddled the ground as I stomped toward the soldiers who would hurt my kingdom.

"Ahh!" a puny male screamed as I gripped his neck and squeezed.

Blood coated my furry hands before bone snapped. I was free and could unleash the rage I'd withheld since my mate had been taken from me. I growled, then lifted my snout to scent the air for her. A body suddenly slammed into mine and the horned gorilla with four arms that had ravaged the villagers in the badlands stood before me. He pounded his broad chest to show he was the superior predator. My fangs bared and I snarled. Finally, something worth fighting. I took a step closer and the gorilla attacked. Four arms tried to grip my torso, teeth snapping at my neck. Little did this creature know, I was the darker beast of another half . . . same body, same mind, same powers, but more savage. My leg lifted in a powerful kick, and I rolled around the gorilla's body to wrap my arms around its waist. I lifted the beast up into the air, then bent my spine slightly backward and the beast tumbled over my shoulder. Quicker than it could regain stability, my pointed fingernails plunged into its chest. Warmth surrounded my hand and I felt the steady beat of a heart. I yanked it out in one solid pull and the hollering animal stared at the bloody heart in my hand for a second, then collapsed to the ground.

I roared and proclaimed myself the apex predator. My hand released the heart and I sniffed the air again for my mate. Instincts declared I find her, claim her, and protect her and our youngling. My ears shifted to the side, then back, to listen for her soothing voice.

"Rune." She called for me, a soft summoning she knew I'd hear from wherever she stood. East. I ran to the east, passing a battleground of frozen soldiers with their fear-stricken faces forever in ice. The Ice Queen and her icy bird continued to freeze the enemy without breaking a sweat.

Then I saw her, my mate. My muzzle curled, and I roared as a male stared at her with hunger for her body and her death. She watched me, and that male behind her instantly became engulfed in flames. Her green eyes scanned my body and I stalked closer. My mate never feared me; she always welcomed me into life. I knew the moment I scented her, she was mine. My other side denied my demand to claim her for too long. Now she is mine, our babe's heart beat strongly in her womb. Her hand touched my chest as I stopped a foot before her. She looked up, and I caressed her cheek with my clean hand.

"I am yours," she whispered and a rumble vibrated inside my chest. War raged around us, and I itched to join the fray, but my mate's safety came first. I would not fail her.

"I'm OK," she eased my discomfort as two female Dramens ran for us with spears. I flung my hand out to will a slice of earth up to fall on top of their soft bodies. Their screams died under the weight of the rock. Instinct told me something was wrong, and I searched my mate for the cause of internal distress signals. Her heart beat within normal rates; her breaths were labored but expected in battle. I shifted my ears to the babe and the heart beat was fast, but I did not feel alarmed.

Something wasn't right. I shifted, growling to show whatever threat neared my mate that I would destroy them. Then I saw them. The two red-armored soldiers the seer had warned about. Verin sought my child, and these dead men walking were part of that plan. I glanced at my mate and wished I could speak like my other side did to convey the severity of the situation. However, she saw it within my eyes and nodded.

"I'll be OK. Do what you have to do. I'll see you soon." She smiled, her hand briefly pressed against her stomach. Fear gripped my heart but I heard nothing wrong. I glanced at Tor who fought nearby and snarled at him. The command was clear. Protect my mate, brother. He nodded and rushed to Sapphira's vicinity. I had two soldiers to eviscerate. I ran to them, gripping enemy bodies as I went and ripping their skulls from their lower jaws. The red-armored men watched me, their eyes darting to Sapphira. Those looks covered my moonlit vision in a blood red haze. Fire danced across the sky as the Desmire spewed his flames over the never-ending army trying to kill my people.

"So, the witch did warn somebody," the soldier to the right muttered, and the other at his side nodded.

"Don't worry. We'll make sure your child is well taken care of as it grows." His hands made a vulgar gesture, and the rage rattled within. I knew their plan was to piss me off, the cursed werewolf they thought no better than a dumb animal. I would then attack and make mistakes. Only I was no mere wolf, I was Rune, the legendary beast who triumphed kingdoms that had disappeared from the maps of history. Ruin and bloodshed were my legacy. They wanted to take the bit of good I actually accomplished in this world. Fuck that.

Their mouths opened wide and long fangs dropped. Their eyes turned red and wings sprouted from their backs. Not Fae then, but it didn't matter. Their wings flapped once and they headed toward me faster than a falcon. I rushed a few feet ahead and skidded low against the earth. Their bodies passed me, and I gripped their ankles. My shoulders ached as their momentum pulled at the joints. I snarled and yanked them back. Their bodies crashed to the ground but they were up in seconds.

The armored men split ways to attack from multiple sides. Their fingernails grew black and long tiny daggers pointed at me. I stomped once, and the ground cracked beneath their feet. It slowed them down but their wings lifted them easily. One of the assholes smirked like it was a great feat to evade my little trick. They obviously didn't know what I was capable of.

They attacked seconds apart, and we clashed in a fight of nails and claws. Pain ripped into my side as a hit found its mark. I roared, and gripped a wing within my hands. My teeth clenched as I ignored the nails that dug into my shoulder muscle. Flesh split as I tore the membranous wing from an armored spine. The male screamed in my ear, and his comrade fought harder. He tried to sink his fangs into my neck, but I took the separated wing and smacked his jaw with it. They fell back, the one hollering in pain as he reached for the opening in his upper back. I slammed my hands into the earth and the ground violently shook. The soldiers reached for each other to again escape whatever rocky trick I'd create. Only this time I played with something new. My other side had an idea and I'd been planning it since Celestine had warned me about these goons. The ground split apart, and the soldiers smirked in the air, knowing they were safe.

"That trick won't harm us," the injured one roared.

Time to see what this body was capable of. My powers shot deep, deep, deep into the core of our planet. Molten rock rolled, and I called it to me. Steam shot up the crevice into the soldier's eyes. They hissed and covered their faces. My other side had wondered if the werewolf could control lava at Verin's palace. Now we both knew we could.

A wall of the molten rock shot into the sky and the red-armored soldiers melted instantly. I pushed the wall toward the advancing enemy. None even had a chance to scream before being smothered by lava. I'd saved my family from Celestine's threat but now a new instinct roared in my mind. I released the lava and let it harden, the melted bodies would remain trapped forever under the rock.

I saw two fallen soldiers in the distance; a familiar tug pulled me closer. As I neared, I sneered at the familiar face of my father with his eyes wide and blood dried at the corner of his lips. His heart did not beat, and I had little remorse for it. My mother slashed her black sword into the torso of a fur-covered Dramen. Her sad eyes collided with mine. I didn't know what to do or how to feel other than indifference. My mother had done as best she could with me but I had become too fucked up to absorb her affections.

"Go be with Sapphira, son." She nudged me on. I followed my mate's scent. She gripped her stomach harshly. Tor tried to help her, but she pushed him back.

"Rune." Her strangled cry had me ready to rip apart the threat. "I thought we had time. Rista said I had at least another week. This pregnancy has gone so fast. I . . ." She gritted her teeth harshly, and a ring of fire and ice and rock surrounded us.

"I think the baby is coming."

Chapter Thirty-Five

Dris

Despite having powerful beings on our side of the war, the enemy's maddening numbers kept coming. They didn't care about self-preservation, only the need to destroy. Hours of pure fighting had passed, and Verin's forces pushed us closer and closer to Crysia's borders. I'd seen Rune impressively pull lava from the earth's core earlier but hadn't seen him since. The moon sat over us, projecting a clear picture of who to kill.

"Dris!" Emrys yelled for me, and I scanned the sea of armored bodies below my wolfhawk. My spider stood in the river; his hands waved for my attention. We swooped down to where he stood, and my beast growled as we landed in the water. He wasn't a fan of the stuff.

"Sapphira needs help. I think she's having the baby, or something is happening." His serious tone made me stretch a hand for his and then help him onto my beast. We took to the sky and avoided the arrows shooting through the air. We searched for our princess. I'd been worried about this happening. Super mama or not, battle caused stress and stress created difficulties during pregnancy. I'd read all the books and talked to Rista to become knowledgeable on the subject.

"There!" My mate pointed at the circle of warriors around the princess. Rune's wolf tore into anyone who dared come close to his mate. The queen sat with her daughter on the ground, while Tor and Nyx completed the other side of their perimeter. We landed in front of them and Nyx sobbed at the sight of our familiar faces. The ground shook as Rune unearthed buried boulders from the ground and threw them at Verin's men.

"Everyone fall back," the queen hollered, and the word spread like wildfire. Our soldiers and allies hauled ass for the safety of Crysia's diamond wall.

"We've got to get her to the palace," I stated and the queen agreed. Desmire dropped to the ground nearby with a loud thud, then shifted. A blue portal appeared near the queen, and I lifted an arrow to my bow. Rika appeared, her white-and-blue hooded cloak covering her face.

"Let's go." The queen jumped into the portal with her advisor. Rune carefully carried his wife through, then Desmire followed. Nyx looked at us after Tor walked through the shimmering portal.

"We'll meet you there," I announced, and we took to the sky on my wolfhawk again.

"Things are not going well at all." I shuddered. Fear I'd never felt before gripped at my chest. My mate's hands squeezed my sides. He knew I wasn't handling things well. Many people had died already. We'd been fighting for eight hours and our people were tired. I glanced to the woods where Verin had sat patiently while his army fought for him. I needed to see where he was and what he was up to before heading to the palace.

"Verin's gone." I tried not to think about the why's of the matter, but a little inkling in my head warned he was after Sapphira. The princess was not going to be fighting any more of this battle. I know many thought she was the chosen one to rid the world of Verin, and maybe she was. As her friends and family, we had to make sure she lived to fight another day. We landed in the garden and raced to Rista's hut where the others were.

"Take her to her room," the healer's normally calm voice shouted, and Rune roared once and ran into the palace. His arms remained steady as he tried not to jostle his mate. We rushed to her room and found Rune mid-shift into his Fae form.

"Sapphira." He clenched his teeth and his body shook from the shift while the moon was still high. She had the power to help him with the change, but that didn't make it easier on his body.

"Let me through," Rista demanded and our small party let her pass. Nyx grasped my arm and I squeezed her tight. Sapphira ran her hand over her stomach and grimaced once. Rista did the same and checked her vitals.

"Your child is not willing to wait until the battle is finished," she declared and Sapphira sobbed.

"Will the baby survive if born now?" I breathed, knowing the child wasn't due right away. Sapphira sobbed, but I saw a gleam in her eyes as she looked directly at me. I'd asked the question she wanted to but couldn't bring herself to mutter.

"Yes. I predicted another week, but there is no reason for any complications. Normally Fae females would be pregnant for a few more weeks. A short pregnancy by many standards, but those wolf genes move things along quicker." She walked into the bathroom. The water sounds echoed around the room as the water flowed into the tub.

"What should we do?" Tor asked, wanting to do something.

"Protect this kingdom so Sapphira can deliver the child without a sword at her throat," the queen demanded and breathed in deep, then exhaled loudly. She was right. Right now, we would only get in the way and possibly cause stress. A war still threatened our lives; we couldn't let them breach the border.

"I'm staying." Rune left no room for argument, and the queen smiled at her son-in-law.

"There is no one better to protect them than you."

His eyes crinkled the slightest before his focus returned to his mate. Desmire kissed his daughter's forehead, then his mate's, and left to fight again. One by one we wished our friend good luck, then rushed outside the palace doors.

"How can we stop them?" Nyx watched as our allies poured in through the opening the queen had allowed in the diamond wall a mile ahead. Tor hugged his mate to soothe the fear in her. Emrys intertwined my fingers with his and a sense of dread settled over us.

"We have to give her time. We can still win this; the war is not over. We only need to change our strategy." I gave myself and the others a pep talk. Thinking is what I did, I just needed to focus on my strengths. Focus on all our strengths.

"Find our ally leaders and bring them here. I think I have a plan and it's gonna take all of us." The thoughts in my head were firing at a rapid pace. This had to work. Sapphira needed this wild plan to work.

Chapter Thirty-Six

Sapphira

Having a baby was a zero out of ten would not recommend. It hurt, and fuck did it hurt bad. Rune stayed by my side, but I knew he also listened to the happenings of the battle outside. Many of our forces were tried to keep the enemy from reaching the diamond wall. If they broke in, that's it. Only the hearts of our people and allies stood between them and destroying Crysia.

"I hate that I'm not out there fighting with them," I mumbled, and Rune shook his head.

"You can't tell me a small part of you doesn't wish you were out striking down Verin's army. Going all psycho werewolf on them." I winced the last word as my womb harshly tightened. Rista eyed me as she talked with my mother.

"I'm right where I want to be. I'll strike down anyone who dares enter this room." Rune lifted my hand to his lips and I swooned.

"First pregnancies tend to take a little longer. All depends on how eager the baby is to join us." Rista walked over and placed a cool cloth on my forehead. I tried sitting in the tub earlier but my powers grew too erratic with pain. I'd nearly boiled myself, then turned the water to ice. Rune got me out of the water before anything worse happened.

"Good to know the next few pregnancies will go smoother." Rune smiled against my hand and I glared at him. He wanted to keep my mind off the pain and aggravating me tended to be the best way. I ignored the chuckles coming from the two other people in the room. Screams echoed against the palace's outer walls, and I winced again. Rune's hand gripped mine a little tighter.

"I'm afraid." I tried to hold onto my bravado, but it cracked hearing people dying so close to home and I couldn't do anything about it.

"My dear daughter. You do not need to be afraid. Right now we must have trust. Verin will not win." My mother's declaration was strong despite the soft tone. I wanted to believe her but given the loss of control on my part in the war, I struggled with trust. Someone knocked on the door and I called them in. Everything I didn't want seen was under a blanket for now.

"Well, Dris officially bought us some time." Nyx walked in first with my other friends behind her. I grinned and was grateful for the distraction.

"What did you do?" I wiggled myself up the stack of pillows. Rune reached out to help me but thankfully I managed on my own. My friends looked like they'd rolled around in mud but tried to clean off before coming into the room. Dried specks decorated their hair.

"We needed to buy time for you to have your baby and our forces to regroup. So we made the terrain a little more difficult for them to trudge through. We created icy patches, then we melted some of them to form huge mud traps. Emrys also snuck into the Hallowstags and aggravated the goblins. So now Verin's army will have to deal with them causing trouble for the soldiers. It won't last forever, but it will help." Dris smiled brightly, so proud of her plan. I laughed and clapped my hands together excitedly. Her plan was brilliant. Maybe that's what we needed to defeat Verin's forces—unexpected surprises. Going head on didn't seem to matter; they kept coming. We needed to fight smarter, not harder. I looked into my mate's icy eyes and knew he thought the same thing.

"I'll be back." He kissed my forehead and stormed out the door. My general needed to speak to his troops. I'd be OK without him for a few minutes.

"So how are you doing?" Nyx stepped forward but kept a few feet between us. She looked OK despite fighting in a war. Her perfect hair was knotted, and a tiny hint of purple under her eyes indicated she needed sleep. They all did.

"I'm OK. The pain comes in waves. Rista said first-time pregnancies can take longer but it all depends on how eager the kiddo is. I sort of hope the babe comes soon, though. It makes me anxious just sitting here while everything is happening." I voiced my thoughts and wished I could have taken them back. Everyone in the room looked at me with a hint of sympathy. They knew how badly I hated being sidelined right now. Emrys stepped closer and eased the tension in the air.

"You're not missing much. Tor and Nyx were making out in the middle of the mud. Then Dris over here kept trying to get me to go all invisible and tie people's shoelaces together." Dris stared at the goat Fae, and laughter burst from my lungs. Tor and Nyx looked everywhere but my eyes and I feel like Emrys's words were true. I knew the feeling, most of the time I fought the urge to kiss my mate, even in the middle of battle.

"I did not do that," Dris huffed and I forgot about my own pity party for a few seconds.

"Thanks, guys. I know I can trust you all to protect Crysia while I'm in here." I looked at my mom, who had mouthed the word "trust" to me. My all-knowing wise mother knew I had the best friends taking care of things and delegating the allies. There was no better group of people for the job than them.

"We love you and Crysia." Dris smiled, and I wished I could hug her. However right now I didn't want to be touched. Every nerve grew increasingly sensitive by the minute.

"We're gonna get back out there, but if you need us, send word." Tor nudged our friends out the door.

My smile slowly shifted to a grimace. I was so over this labor already. I said bye and they waved as they left. Rista strode to my bedside and proceeded to check how my body was doing.

"You're doing really well. The key is staying as calm as you can." She breathed calmly, and I tried to mirror her breaths. I could do this. I had control over myself and how I reacted to this situation.

"Well done, little gem." My heart rate spiked as Verin stood in the doorway. Mother rushed for him but she wasn't fast enough. His hand rested in front of his face, then he blew hard and black dusted covered the room. She crumpled to the ground, gasping for air, her wide eyes on me. Rista collapsed seconds later, and I threw fire toward him to which he dodged. My throat tickled but I didn't seem to be affected the way the others were. I summoned fire, ice, and earth to wipe this man off the face of the planet, but they fizzled upon my fingertips.

"The dust was laced with a power sedative. Can't have you melting me to the floor before the baby is born. Since you have a bit of my power, it doesn't knock you out like them." He stood close to the bed, but not close enough to where I could reach him.

"You've caused so much trouble for me, little gem. But yet, I find myself glad I spared your life. You and that cursed beast created a gift, one I will raise to bless the world with dark power. The Heart Tree essence in one being. That sort of power cannot be extinguished. It must be molded and shaped for the greater good of the world. My world. But don't worry, I'm not going to kill you yet. Hurting you could harm the child within you," he crooned, and tears cascaded down my cheeks. His hand struck out to grasp mine, and the veins beneath my skin turned purple. The pain in my womb instantly doubled.

"Time is of the essence, little gem. I'm here to claim my gift." His vile lips lifted unnaturally toward his eyes. Pure undiluted agony burned through my body as whatever Verin forced into my body sped up the process of birth from hours to merely minutes.

Chapter Thirty-Seven

Rune

I stood just outside the palace walls with Najen and something felt wrong. My brother had left Sapphira's room moments ago, and they said all was well. My beast roared, and I was tempted to allow the moon to take control of me again. Desmire landed in the garden, then shifted. Once Fae again, his eyes collided with mine and I knew for certain despite the calm appearance in Crysia right now, something was very wrong. My feet whirled around, and I raced up the stairs to my wife, Desmire right behind me, a sword in his hand. Sapphira's screams tore through the halls and my heart squeezed. I kicked open the door and roared. Verin sat beside my mate. Tears and sweat coated her red face from so much pain. The palace shook with my rage but a hand landed on my shoulder. Verin watched the dragon and I with a wicked grin on his face.

"You be with Sapphira, I'll take care of him." The calmness in the dragon's voice masked the violent anger that made his hand tremor the slightest.

"Hello, Brother," Verin greeted us, his eyes darted to the two bodies on the floor and I bit my cheek so hard, the skin broke. My queen and Rista lay on the floor. They still breathed but appeared paralyzed. Verin stood slowly. His hand reached out to pat my wife's head twice. She glared at him with all the fire inside of her struggling to melt him. He must have subdued her as well, otherwise he'd be nothing but ash. I wanted to fight him. I wanted to smear the earth with his blood. But my mate needed me. Her screams tore through me with each passing second. I'd failed her in the past. I wasn't there to protect her as a human, I couldn't help her in the desert, but I could be there for her now. I slowly stepped to the side for Desmire to step into the room. While the brothers entered a death stare, my feet moved quietly to my wife. My eyes watched every movement the other men made, as I approached the bed. Sapphira gripped my hand and tears poured heavily down her cheeks.

"I . . ." She tried to speak but her sob became a pain-filled scream.

"What a delightful family gathering," Verin mused while his hand pulled a red blade from his scabbard.

"I will not let you hurt my family." Desmire squatted down to touch his mate's cheek. She was immobilized but breathing. The dragon stood, his gray gaze on the enemy. They circled around each other in the middle of the room.

"I was quite surprised to find out the princess was yours and not mine. She was too good to be mine. I should have known from the beginning. But at least I got to sit on the throne that was meant for you and fuck your mate." Verin's snickered attempts to rattle the dragon didn't pierce the man's leather armor to reach their true target. Desmire and the queen loved each other despite their tragedies. Verin never got the piece of her that mattered most to a mate—her heart and soul.

"Rune, I'm scared," Sapphira managed to hiss before her back bowed and her eyes pinched together. I didn't know what to do to help her. I'd never delivered a baby before.

"Time to die, brother. For good." Verin's grin fell as he realized his taunts didn't blind his brother. With his sword gripped tightly in his hands, he rushed for Desmire.

"Rune, you need to watch for the baby." A whisper caught my attention and I looked at Rista lying on the floor. Her eyes watched me. Her mouth moved, but no one else seemed to notice. My werewolf hearing did, though. I nodded as Rista did the one thing she could to help me. Step by step she guided me through what I needed to do for Sapphira and our child. Desmire moved the battle with Verin into the halls, and I heard their clashed swords clang against the stone walls.

"Sapphira, listen to me. I don't know what he did, but you are fierce and I know you can bring this baby into the world." I hoped my words gave her comfort and the will to fight. She shook her head from side to side.

"I'm here, wife, I'm here and I won't let him hurt our family," I vowed and removed the blanket to watch for the baby's head. I breathed deep to calm my nerves that suggested I would somehow fuck this up.

"If you can see the baby's head, then she needs to push," Rista murmured, and I looked into my mate's eyes.

"You need to push now, Sapphira. I'm here. I'm with you. You can do this. Push, Sapphira." I guided my mate as her fingers gripped the sheets and she clenched her teeth. Slowly the baby began to move. I smiled, my terror and joy mingled into one.

"You're doing it. Keep going, Sapphira." I gripped her hand and waited per Rista's instructions to catch our child. After many roaring and excruciating pushes, Sapphira gave one last battle cry into the room and our daughter was born. Tears fell onto my cheeks as I took the little babe in my hands. Brown skin like her mother, black hair like mine, and a scream to rival her mother's. My wife collapsed onto the bed, her pain diminishing immensely with the child out. I quickly made work of the cord and wrapped the child in a blanket that had been set at the end of the bed, all per Rista's coaching.

"You gave us a daughter, wife," I breathed and held the crying child to her. She smiled and broke into gentle sobs. I started to worry she was in pain again but she smiled through the tears. Happy tears.

"Hi, baby," she whispered, and I couldn't stop smiling. We had a child, a daughter. A beautiful daughter. Her eyes opened the slightest and Sapphira gasped. Smokey gray eyes just like her grandfather's greeted us. I helped Sapphira adjust the pillows to sit more upright and placed our babe in her arms.

"She's perfect." She placed a kiss on the babe's little head.

"He ran away. Coward." Desmire's voice entered the room, and we turned both our tear-filled, joyful faces to him.

"Well done, you two," he congratulated us then scooped his wife up to lay her on the bed next to Sapphira. The queen gently cried with the rest of us as she watched her grandbaby. Her fingers flexed as she fought for control over her body again. Whatever Verin used was wearing off. Desmire then picked Rista up and set her in a chair nearby. She whispered a checklist for me to look over the baby, and I did without voicing my actions. The baby looked fine as far as I could tell.

"Look at her eyes," Sapphira stated, her arms lifted upward for Desmire to take the child. The dragon cradled the baby in his big arms so gently. I knew what this moment meant to him—a second chance to be with his family, to spoil his grandchild, and to teach her everything he knew. Mostly, he would spoil her and protect her with every ounce of essence within him.

"She looks like you when you were a baby." He caressed the babe's rounded cheeks and pouty lips. They seemed to stare into each other's eyes, possibly the recognition of another dragon or beast behind her perfect face. Then her little mouth opened and cries blared from those small but powerful lungs.

"She's got a mouth like you, too," Desmire said, and suddenly an arrow's tip protruded through his chest. He groaned, closed his eyes, then opened them as the pain registered.

Chapter Thirty- Eight

Rune

"Perfect timing," Verin spat through a bloody mouth in the doorway, having slithered from wherever he had hidden, ready to strike at this vulnerable moment with a bow in his hand. The babe screamed, and Desmire lowered her to Sapphira's waiting arms.

"Father . . ." her voice broke with the sight of the injured dragon.

"Rune, get Sapphira and the baby out of here. I'll handle this." The man whirled around just as another arrow buried deep in his stomach.

"No!" Sapphira screamed in terror and despair. I scooped her up inside the sheet beneath her and willed the wall behind me to shatter. Stone tumbled to the ground and a great opening gave way to the fresh air of the night.

"That child is mine!" Verin bellowed, but Desmire stopped him from reaching us. Fists connected, the men grappled, and Verin fought to take a step closer but Desmire would not yield one inch.

"Get them out of here. Go!" Desmire commanded, and I stared into his gray eyes. The same one's my daughter now honored him with. Blackness seeped into his veins as he pinned Verin to the ground. He might have survived the arrows, but poison was fatal. He was dying, and yet he had enough fight in him to let us escape.

"Go," he mouthed, and I glanced at the queen for a second as she watched her mate die.

"Go," he commanded again, his eyes soft, and a feigned smile took over his face.

"I love you all so much," he whispered. His eyes met mine, then Sapphira's, then settled on his mate's. From one father to another, he showed me what true sacrifice meant. A father would give anything for his family. He'd give his love, his strength, his devotion. He would die to protect his family. My family. I nodded to the man who was more a father than my own, then jumped through the broken wall. My wife sobbed for her father with our child safely in her arms as I willed the earth to softly meet my feet.

"I'm sorry," I whispered to my wife as I raced us far away from the palace to the safety of the Hallowstags. I let my werewolf instincts come forward to listen or sense danger nearby. Nothing. We were deep into the woods and not even a bird chirped in the trees. A safe haven for my mate's wails to reach high levels. I held them both as I sank to the ground.

"Sapphira, the baby." My wife's head shifted to look at our child who nuzzled her for milk. She did what Rista taught her, and our daughter latched on with ease. I sighed, thankful something went right.

"I'm sorry about your father. He was a great male." I didn't know how to comfort her. This loss would cut deep, and there was no battle stitch I knew to sew the pieces back together.

"It's not fair. After everything he's been through. He finally got to be a real part of our lives. He has a grandchild now to love, and it's just not OK. I'm not OK," she sobbed. One arm cradled our babe and the other tugged at my shirt.

"He did what any real father would do. He protected those he loved, and he loved you, your mother, and our child more than anything in all the realms." I bit back tears as his sad knowing face popped into my head. My arms stayed strong around her weeping body until long after the babe fell asleep with a full belly. I looked up to the purple and orange sky as the sun brightened our dark night.

"I'm very sorry for your loss my dear." Celestine's voice echoed against the trees of the forest. My head shifted to find the seer, but she hadn't arrived in spirit form yet.

"Celestine?" Sapphira sniffled, and I readied my powers just in case it turned into a trick.

"Meow-hoo." Her pet walked by us and I exhaled. My body sagged against the tree I'd leaned against. The seer appeared seconds later. Her shimmering corporeal body stood three feet away from us, her hood pushed back to reveal her big owlish eyes and black hair.

"Desmire's fate has always been of triumph and tragedy. However, if given the chance, he would do it all over again. The journey was worth seeing you grow to be the powerful daughter he knew you would be." Celestine waved her hand and two cups of tea appeared before us. Sapphira reached for the wooden cup closest to her and downed the liquid quickly. Her tremors ceased and her tears slowly decreased. I sipped from my cup and nothing but the flavor of lavender hit my senses. Celestine chuckled.

"Yours is normal lavender tea. No additives." She smiled and my eyes rolled. It soothed my dry throat so I kept drinking.

"I assume you're here for a reason?" I asked.

"Verin will still come for the child, but he will not get her. You defeated the red soldiers. Had you not killed them they would have been there with the evil king and overpowered you and the dragon instantly. To save your daughter and to end this war, you must give the child to me, to protect until it is over." Sapphira's calm posture turned rigid as Celestine spoke those last few words.

"We just had her. She hasn't even been in this world for a few hours, and I'm supposed to give her over?" Her voiced raised an octave and I wondered if she'd strike the seer. The woman only nodded her head.

"What will you do with her while you end this horrid war? Strap her to your back? I am the guardian of the Heart Tree, and now I am the guardian for your daughter. I will always be there for her, to help her when she needs me. Right now, she needs you to defeat Verin and rid this realm from his darkness once and for all."

A shiver rolled up my spine. Destiny always had big plans for Sapphira. We also understood that by killing the Heart Tree, our daughter would have an even greater destiny. Celestine's next words mirrored my thoughts, and I hugged Sapphira closer.

"It is your destiny to end this and bring a new light upon the future for both Fae and humans. The secrets and the truths all led to this—the grand destiny for the princess with a sapphire core. You must rise, Sapphira, rise for your family, to honor your father's sacrifice and usher us into the new age of love and peace."

My mate shifted her head to look at me. Fear, hope, sadness, and love all swirled in her beautiful eyes. She wanted an answer from me, and there was only one to give. If she turned a cold shoulder to destiny, then we'd lose everything. I nodded and angled my head to press my lips to hers.

"OK." The teacup in her hand refilled with a blue liquid.

"Drink up, my dear. That tea will heal your body and replenish your well of powers. We can't have you heading back to battle feeling like you just gave birth now, can we?" Celestine floated over to us and held her hands out for the child. Sapphira drank

221

her new tea, her face scrunched up from the taste. I kissed my daughter's forehead, and Sapphira whispered our love. Hesitantly, my wife placed our sleeping babe in Celestine's suddenly physical arms. She whimpered slightly, and the seer hummed. Her body slowly swayed to soothe the child back to a peaceful sleep.

"I will bring her to you when it's done." The seer disappeared with our daughter. Sapphira breathed deep, her hands clutching me tightly. My chest ached from the babe's absence.

"Let's end this war together." Sapphira crawled out of my lap to stand in new, clean clothes and armor. Her strength and body were perfectly healed, like she hadn't given birth at all. Part of me hated that and wanted to see her pregnant again, but that would wait. One day, if she wanted to at all. If not, then I would forever be grateful to have been blessed with our daughter.

"Together." I held my hand out for hers. Our essence and resolve pounded in our hearts. Time to pay back Verin for the pain he'd caused.

Together.

Chapter Thirty-Nine

Emrys

Word spread around the battlefield about Desmire's death. Soldiers had burst into Sapphira's room to find the dragon dead, the queen and healer paralyzed. They searched the palace but Rune, Sapphira, and the baby were gone. Every person felt the devastation from the pain the family was going through. Dris rambled random facts for the past hour. It was either that or give into the dark sadness that crept over the people fighting for Crysia.

Was the war over? Had we already lost and just didn't realize it yet?

"My queen." Someone nearby spoke into the tense air. Our group whirled around to see the queen stomp down the path from the palace doors. Her murderous face stained with tears told the truth of her mate's death. Now she wanted revenge. No advisor, no allied queen could stop her as two diamond swords grew from her palms.

"Oh, no," Dris whispered, and the ground trembled. The diamond wall stood between her and the enemies attempting to get inside.

"Everybody get down!" the Ice Queen bellowed seconds before the whole north side of the diamond wall exploded. Queen Olyndria roared raw and deep, her power matching the need for revenge. The shards of diamonds flew into the bodies of the enemy, tearing flesh and impaling them through their armor. The diamonds reached thousands of the evil army. Their groans and screams of pain filled the air, but none were louder than the grief that poured from the queen's every movement.

She marched onto the blood-soaked fields with the two shimmering swords in her hand, straight for the enemy who still grasped at the reality that destroyed their soldiers. Verin fucked up. He had cut too deep, too wide, and now the broken had a drive to retaliate. From the corner of my eyes, two forms ran from the Hallowstags. Sapphira and Rune ran mere feet behind the queen. Rage and fury fueled every powerful step closer to clash with an army of red and black. The sight inspired every heart in pain to stand up and run behind them with icy fingers shaking with fear . . . straight into the line of Dramens. I pulled Dris by the arm to collide with me and kissed her deep.

"I love you," I said, then released her to run into the fray. Powers clashed and bodies dropped as the royals unleashed their pain. The ground opened up and bodies scrambled to get out of the way, only to find an ice stake embedded in their skulls. The three of them eviscerated anyone who came within a hundred-foot radius. Our forces joined them with renewed motivation, and the enemy couldn't find a strategy to stop us. I turned invisible and sliced into unsuspecting soldiers. Dramens with guns fired in every direction without care if they hit friends or foes. One by one we pushed their forces back. The battle cries from our leaders fed our fight . . .

Until I saw them. Every person fighting for Crysia and freedom froze. Giants, the large men from the mountains of the far north, stomped closer. A hundred of them, covered in armor, over two hundred feet tall, walked with the remains of Verin's army. Not even power, rage, or strategy could defeat them.

Chapter Forty

Dris

When Rune had mentioned Desmire's roar for legendary creatures to come help, I thought that would be great. I'd read about so many beings of this realm that could work with us to defend Crysia. Even the phoenix took out a ton of soldiers. Their army fought with pride of battling alongside that bird. But the legendary giants of the mountains from the corners of our continent were not here to help defend the kingdom. They were here to destroy it.

We were able to take down ten out of the hundred. The Dramens and soldiers used the distraction of our most powerful Fae fighting the giants to gain traction and breach our city. Houses and shops burned. The flames and smoke turned my beautiful home into a nightmare. Soldiers burst into the palace. They raided, smashed, and set fire to everything. Like a plague of locusts, they left nothing in their wake but devastation.

"No!" I rushed into the palace to save my precious home. The symbol of our kingdom, the diamond leafed tree behind the throne, shattered on the floor. No rainbows danced across the room, only shattered hope and dreams. Smoke filled the air and a feeling the size of a boulder dropped in my gut. I raced for my library. Hands shook as I sliced two men with torches, watching my precious safe haven blaze with the tinder of knowledge.

"Help!" I screamed. Maybe someone had the power to help. The flames grew wild and in a matter of minutes, I knew there was no chance to save my library. Paint boiled on the art-covered roof. The stained-glass windows shattered, and I had no choice but to flee. The whole building shook. I raced for the door just as a giant with large gray legs and huge tusk-like knives in his hands slashed at the palace. Chunks of wood and stone fell to the ground, and I jumped out of the way before being squished.

I saw my friends fighting in the distance, but no one could do anything. We'd lost. Verin won. On my hands and knees, I scrambled away just as another giant joined in smashing the palace. Our citizens were safe in the shelter, but for how long? Verin knew about it as the once king of Crysia. The age of darkness gripped tighter at our throats.

We'd lost. We'd lost.

"Hey, pretty girl," said a man with black paint on his face, black tattoos around his eyes, and piercings on his eyebrows and lips. Four more men and one woman surrounded me. Dramens. I had no weapon to fight them off. I'd be able to fight one at a time with my hands but not all of them. Rough hands gripped my arms. Icy fingers wrapped around my hair, but I kept my scream inside. They wanted my fear and my screams to fuel their lust. My feet kicked. I reached up to dig my fingers into sensitive places, but a knife bit into my throat.

"Easy girl, we just want to have a little fun." The man holding my hair laughed, and the others joined in.

A loud squeal blared and echoed across the land. The Dramens dropped me to the ground to cover their ears. All eyes turned to the little creature with crystals on his backs stood before us, his crystals glowing in the sunlight. Lucky!

"I smell barbeque." One of the men laughed and pointed his knife toward the little creature. Blinding light flared from his back. Instantly, I curled into myself on the ground, hands over my face as Lucky released his power on the Dramens. The scent of melted flesh and bone filled my nostrils, but I didn't release my hands until the sound of the exploding radiation of the creature ceased to nothing.

Finally, after a minute or two, I looked up to see Lucky with his snout raised, defender of his home. Gasps echoed around the ruins of the palace. Tears of awe replaced the sadness on my cheeks as I stared behind him. Out of the Hallowstags walked creatures big and small. Unicorns, with their hooves stomping the dirt. Nearly fifty of them stood at the tree line. Goblins, deer with golden horns, fifteen Catagaro like Cara, and bears of all sizes stepped into view beside them, each focused on the enemies of this realm. Lucky squealed again and the evil soldiers around me laughed despite what Lucky had done to the Dramens close to me. They didn't know or understand what was happening.

Suddenly, a thunderous roar tore through the skies, and the ground vibrated. I looked for Sapphira's dragon but saw her in Fae form staring at the sky. Eight massive beasts flew over the snowy peaks of the mountains. Dragons.

My hands gripped at my hair. I sat on the ground in shock as creatures, legendary and all, unleashed their wrath upon the darkness that threatened their world. Fire rained down on the battlefield. Talons gripped into the giants as the dragons flapped their great wings. The giants were lifted off the ground and dropped from high heights. Unicorns trampled soldiers and stabbed them with their horns. The horrendous water creatures crawled from the river with their big eyes and sharp teeth. Their fish-like lower halves wiggled on the ground as they grabbed every enemy they could sink their claws into. The mermaids that frequented the Hallowstags were in the river, too, throwing rocks at the army.

From fire and ruin, the beings of this realm made their stand. I stood ready to fight alongside them. The giants tried to fight back against the dragons, but they either lost their life or fled. Dramens and Verin's soldiers scurried about. They ran from the creatures that hunted them, and our soldiers took no prisoners.

Desmire's call to the realm was heard. Every creature I'd ever read about had answered him, to fight, to defend, and to save our world.

Chapter Forty -One

Sapphira

Dragons and all the creatures of this realm had answered my father's plea for aide. Whether they knew it or not, they honored his sacrifice by rescuing our kingdom. I knew I'd never witness a collaboration like this in the face of darkness for the rest of my immortal life. A legend was born right here and now. Centuries from now would tell the story of the great battle of Crysia. Dragons, unicorns, great beasts, and animals fought alongside the Fae to defeat evil.

I even saw the fish creature that tried to eat me when I was human. This world was worth saving. A man on a giant three-headed snake slithered ahead, commanding his forces to turn around and fight. They ignored him and rushed for the mountains.

"Listen to your king!" Lethirya commanded, the Dramen royals shouting similar words at their people. Defeat teetered on the tip of a blade.

"Rune!" I called to my mate and he pulled his black blade out of the red-and-black armor of a soldier's torso. My head shifted to the shouting leaders, and he understood. "Let's go get them. It's payback time."

Lethirya's eyes narrowed at our ascension on their position. Verin searched for the babe on me and saw none. A sneer marred his face when he realized she wasn't with me and that my body had healed. He knew he'd never take my child from me now. His army deserted him, and his victory slipped from his fingers. Wind and sand whirled toward us, but Rune sliced into the rotation of the tornado with a sheet of heavy earth. He moved to the Dramen king and queen with a snarl. The ground splintered around them, and lava boiled over the cracks. My powerful mate, master of earth.

"You just don't know how to die, do you?" my cousin screamed and rushed at me with a new beast, teeth barred to chomp. I flexed my hands and two whips made of flames flowed free. Just before her reptile-like creature could slam its heavy jaws on my head, I jumped out of the way and snapped the whip at her. One tip caressed her cheek, leaving a red-and-black cauterized mark on her skin. The other wrapped around her arm. My hands yanked on the line, and she tumbled off her ride. She screamed as living, burning fire seared into her arm. With my free whip, I whirled around and snapped it again. It coiled around her neck and I stared into her eyes as she knew I would let the fire burn her head right off. She thrashed on the ground to unwind the flames.

In an instant, I snuffed them out. She scrambled to move her hand. The spark of a portal grew, and I laughed. Rock rose from beneath her and covered her hands. With her wrists and fingers encased in the stable ground, she writhed, unable to fight back.

"You just don't know how to die, do you cousin?" I smirked. Half tempted to crush her skull beneath my boot, a sudden blow to the stomach knocked me back, and Lethirya was set free.

"Lethirya, finish her." Verin's snake's tail had slammed into me.

As if on cue, my cousin's creature ran at me. I dug my feet into the ground, ready to jump. Light grew in my hands and I formed them into balls against my palms. The beast's eyes narrowed and I threw the light balls at its eyes. Blinded and burned, it lunged and I jumped up and willed a sword of ice to grow from my hands. As my body descended, so did my blade on the creature's neck. Lethirya screamed and brought her red sword down hard at my head. My ice sword thwarted the sword and shattered. I rolled away as her frantic attempts to take me down hit at rapid speed. She laughed, she screamed, and she fought like a madwoman. Her mind had shattered some time ago. Part of me pitied her, but not enough. My fingers dug into the ground, and her feet sank six inches into the dirt. As she swung her sword around like an old windmill, I stood tall and strong. I opened my mouth and roared with all the strength of a dragon. Fire spewed from my lips, scorching her for a second. I breathed in deep and felt something hard grow in my palm . . . a hatchet of pure sapphire.

"Die!"

She groaned and wiggled out of the dirt with her boots trapped in the earth. Barefoot with blood marks on her face, she raised her sword for a killing shot. I spun around as her blade whizzing past my ear and slammed the axe into her chest, through her evil heart. I vaguely heard Verin yell for his daughter, but I stood there to watch the light leave her eyes.

"You . . ." A rage-filled voice entered the vicinity. I released my hold on the hachet and Lethirya's lifeless body crumpled to the ground. My mother had sliced Verin's snake in two, and now stood before him with her dual diamond swords, ready to exact revenge.

My mate battled with the king of the Dramens. The queen lay dead on the ground, her neck slashed and red blood flowing freely from the wound. Rune would cleanse this world of Harold, and the Dramens would be no more. Without a leader to follow, and their numbers down to double digits they would disappear into the history pages.

"You mated the weaker brother. Poor choice, wife." Verin gripped a sword between his slimy, evil hands. Blades clashed, and the battle for the end began. Taking advantage of my hatchet, I whirled it full speed at Verin's chest, but he knocked it away with his blade. I scanned the dead around me for something familiar. Two guns, an axe, and a bow lay beside a group of bodies. I vaguely considered taking Lethirya's sword but didn't know if it was booby-trapped. Honestly, I wouldn't put it past the nasty woman to do something like that.

First, I picked up the gun even though I didn't know how it worked. However, once I saw it had no bullets inside it, I picked up an axe. The head instantly fell off the handle and I growled. What the hell was wrong with these guy's weapons? No better than toys.

Next was the bow. Its wood remained sturdy in my hands, the string pulled tight, but I couldn't find an arrow in the vicinity.

A gurgled groan came from my right and Rune had his blade buried in the Dramens' king's chest. Blood bubbled out from his gaped mouth as my mate pressed his boot onto the king's stomach and removed him from the blade with one powerful kick.

Arrow, arrow, arrow. I needed an arrow. My mother grunted as she wielded those swords like an extension of herself. Verin was evil, and evil didn't fight honorably. He was going to cheat or fight dirty. Just as I thought it, he rolled his body to the ground. His fingers grabbed a handful of dirt and threw it straight into my mother's eyes.

"Ah!" she screamed and wiped at her eyes.

Screw it. I used my essence to create an arrow from my core. Blue sapphire gleamed in the sun's light as I docked it to the bow. My lungs expanded with my deep inhale, but I didn't release right away. The man who raised me stood to his full height. He'd never showed me unconditional love or true kindness. Only when I acted proper did he give me sincere words. The monster with a sinister grin on his face had ruined so much of my life. His desire to rule destroyed the lives of millions of humans, Fae, my family. He slowly stepped closer to my mother, light on his feet. She swung her swords blindly, but he avoided them with ease. Seconds passed, she winced, then blinked over and over in his direction. With an outstretched hand, a black liquid coated the king's fingertips. Poison.

My mother's breaths evened, and before he could touch her, she lunged in his direction, catching him off guard. I released the air in my lungs and the arrow. It flew straight and true right into the exposed chest of the evil king. He gasped. He collapsed to his knees as he clutched at the sapphire arrow sticking out of his armor. Black-and-red liquid seeped from his lips with an expression of disbelief on his evil face.

A warm hand landed on my shoulder. My mate, my husband. It was over. My mother rose. With her eyes clean of debris, she stepped to the dying king, crossed her swords on the sides of his neck, and then swiped her arms wide. Verin's head severed between the dual blades and the last of his dark legacy fell to the bloody battlefield.

Chapter Forty-Two

Sapphira

I couldn't do anything but stare at the broken body of Verin on the ground. We'd been fighting for this ending for so long that I still waited for him to trick us. Like just kidding, that was my body double, I'm over here and will ruin your lives. But he didn't move. My mother stood above him, not moving, either. Maybe she felt the same. Slowly, I rose to my feet and trudged to her. There were no words to ease the pain we both felt. Even the evil king's death didn't soothe the ache. The ground shook as a massive beast landed on the battlefield behind us. Mother continued to stare at the body, then looked off at the mountain. I breathed deeply, then turned to face the dragon that wanted an audience.

"You have the heart of a dragon." The dark blue dragon was larger than any creature I'd ever seen. His low timbered voice echoed in my head.

"My father was blessed with the essence of a dragon." My throat burned with the threat of tears speaking about him, and the dragon's head lowered slightly.

"We felt one of our own return to the sky. I am sorry for your loss."

I wiped the tears that fell despite my fight to hold them off.

"We'd been called to aid in many wars. The affairs of Fae never stray into our existence, until now. Your father's call was like that of our ancient one. The Onyx dragon. We came to honor that spirit." The dragon's head lifted to full height and for the first time in what felt like days, I smiled.

"Thank you." I couldn't find any other words to say. I know my father would have loved to have seen these magical beasts set fire to the enemy. We had changed the tide of the battle because of my father's plea. The dragons and all the creatures had come. Without them, it would have been over.

"If you have need of us again, we will come. Our numbers are so few, and I sense two dragon essences here. We protect each other." He lowered his head once more. His large blue wings flapped once, and the wind cooled the sweat on my face.

"How shall I call you if I do not know your name?" I asked, knowing I probably had to roar in some way like my father did. The beast huffed, much like another dragon I knew did.

"My name is Valor, prince of dragons." He puffed his chest before his body lifted higher and higher off the ground. The other seven dragons flew in line behind him as their bodies disappeared over the mountain peaks.

"Wife," Rune's voice came from my right and I faced him. His arms opened and I ran into them instantly. So many emotions from relief to hope and despair overcame me. He held me through them all, my solid rock on shaky ground. Soft steps approached, and I peeked from Rune's chest to see my mother. Rune dared to open his arms wider and my mother hesitated for the barest of moments, then stepped into our comfort. She needed support now more than ever. My badass mom's tears fell and bless my husband did not flinch at being the stronghold of our meltdown.

"I love you both," she murmured, and she stepped back from our embrace.

"I love you," I told her, and Rune nodded his sentiments. A smile didn't grace her lips but I knew she needed time. The grief did not end with swift justice.

"Let's go home," Rune mumbled against my ear and I nodded. Not that we had much of a home left. The palace was burned and broken. The city lay in rubble. As we walked to our shattered kingdom, we passed so much death. I didn't know how to overcome so much destruction and pain that lay on the road ahead.

"Sapphira!" Nyx's face came into view as we neared the once diamond wall. She looked like shit, and Tor wasn't any better off behind her. Rune and I refused to unclasp hands as she embraced me. The thought of separating right now seemed unbearable.

"Are you guys all right?" After a quick scan with my free hand, I detected no injury that couldn't heal with a little rest.

"Yeah, we're OK. Dris is fine, she's by the palace with Emrys. He is not doing great. Rista said he's gonna live but . . ." She searched for the words, and I didn't have the patience to wait for them. Rune and I rushed up the cracked cobblestone road to where a frantic Dris paced next to Emrys who sat on the ground. Blood caked the tips of hair on the left side of his head. He winced as Rista touched it with some green goo.

"Are you OK?"

"I'm fine. Emrys has lost his hearing. Other than that he's ok," Dris blurted from her line of pacing.

"I'm sorry about your father and your home, and everything. I'm sorry we couldn't fight them off better." Dris burst into tears and I pulled her into my chest.

"I'm glad you're still with me. I'm glad Emrys has you. No better person to help him than you." I squeezed her tight. Part of me wished I had better words to soothe her pain, but I didn't. I couldn't say "It's ok" because it wasn't.

"At least the shelter wasn't breached. Our reinforcements came at the right time."

My people had survived. Not all, but as long as hearts beat in our kingdom, Crysia would survive. Emrys stood a moment later and pulled Dris to him. He couldn't hear her freaking out but he could see it. They needed time. Hell we all did.

"Wait? Where's the baby?" Dris popped her head away from Emry's chest. My lungs squeezed and Rune's body stilled beside me. Celestine. The battle was over. We needed our child back. I needed to see her, smell her, touch her. Make sure she was real and not a fantasy.

"She's right here." Celestine's soft voice flowed through the air. Rune and I turned, our hands separated. Celestine stood three feet away, our babe cradled in her arms.

"She slept the whole time. Truly a perfect baby." The seer closed the distance and gently placed the babe in my arms.

She yawned and her little eyes with long black lashes opened. I nearly wept seeing those smoky gray eyes. A piece of my father lived on and if Valor had been right, I had a feeling a dragon's essence danced with the ruby core inside her.

"You did it, my dear. A new era of love and peace has arrived." Celestine grinned, her large eyes scanned the scene before me.

"It doesn't feel spectacular yet," I mumbled, although every look into my daughter's eyes made me feel more hopeful.

"A part of me wishes I would have known the outcome," I whispered as Rune's finger reached up to caress the babe's cheeks. Her little hand grasped his finger tightly.

"The journey is the best part. If you knew the end result would have led you right back to this palace, then why would you have left it?" Celestine grinned, her words soaked beneath my skin.

"You left to learn, to grow, to experience, and change your life. The princess standing before me now has come into her own. There is no amount of treasure or materials that matter more than being alive. That is the true treasure and true purpose for every being's existence. We are meant to live, Sapphira. To feel joy, to feel sadness, to learn, and feel alive. Your kingdom has felt loss, but you have been given the chance to keep breathing. As long as you can do that, you can help shape this world into a better one." The seer winked, then floated away. Of course, in the end she had a point. Everything I'd experience, every single bit of it led me to here. Rune, Dris, Emrys, Tor, Nyx, their choices, their own fates all joined to bring them to this moment.

I looked at my babe, my mate, my friends, and my kingdom but this time I had a gratefulness in my heart. We were broken, we were hurting, but we were alive. I wouldn't take that for granted.

Chapter Forty-Three

Sapphira

Days passed, and I'd barely slept. People immediately got to work rebuilding Crysia. We slept in tents wherever we could put them at night. I'd worked with my mother and the rulers from the other kingdoms to sort out the dead. They would be transported with the help of Rika to their families to be handled with how they wanted. We'd buried and burned as many as we could from our own kingdom. The fires brought many tears and sobs for loved ones. I tried to stay strong for my people, but when little flowers that usually grew on the graves beside the mountains spread across the meadow, I lost it. The unity stars ushered in a new beauty to a dark place.

My father was given a send-off in a way I thought he'd like best . . . with dragon fire. Flowers covered every inch of his pyre. My mother stayed by his resting place until the sun rose the next day. She barely spoke to anyone beyond duties as queen. The only time I saw her smile was when she held the baby. Rune and I hadn't talked about her name since that one night before battle. Maybe that made us bad parents but we just had too much to do and her name needed to be thought upon.

"Sapphira." My mother startled me out of my thoughts as I looked at the vast sight of the tiny pink-and-white lilies covering the ground. It almost looked like scatterings of snow on the ground if you squinted.

"Before our allies leave, I'm crowning you as queen." I whirled around to look at her face. I did not expect those words nor the determination and pride on her face.

"Mother, I don' think I'm—

She cut me off with a wave of her hand. "This world has been cleansed of the old. It's new, and it will be beautiful. But it won't be me leading our people into this new era. It has to be you. You were always meant to be the queen who united the realms and brought peace." A tiny portion of her lips lifted, her hand reached out to clasp mine. All I could do was stare at her. Me, the queen of Crysia?

"You are deserving of a wonderful life, Sapphira. I did everything I could to guide you, to help you, even when I was not myself. You've become more than I ever imagined. I'm so proud of you. Your father is so proud of you too." She cried and I couldn't seem to stop myself from doing it as well. She hugged me tight, then left me at the meadow. Eventually, my stomach growled and I walked back to camp. My friends sat in a circle by a fire with plates of food. Rune had our babe tucked into his chest with a makeshift wrap the Ice Queen showed him how to operate. Those two had connected in their understanding of silence. Kunsula sat beside Dris, the two of them talking quietly. Kuanish had died on the battlefield and his twin sister was not doing well. Tor comforted his mother, and my heart squeezed knowing that they would be leaving me soon. Technically Rune was the firstborn, heir to the throne of Regno Dei Lupi. However, he handed the rights over to Tor. When asked if he would come home, he simply shrugged and stated this was his home.

"There you are. We heard the news. You are going to be a great queen." Nyx clapped her hands as she noticed me and the others looked up. Emrys followed those gazes and smiled big.

"Takes a great queen to know one," I teased, and she blushed. Nyx would become a queen as well in the near future. A little whimper came from Rune's chest and the babe squirmed.

"She heard your voice and wants you." Rune unwrapped the babe and held her out for me. Rune may not have had a good father role model, but he stepped up and was the best father I could ever want for our babe. As soon as I pulled her to my chest, she nuzzled for food. Hungry little creature.

"Are you ever gonna pick a name for her?" Tor asked, and I looked to Rune.

"Desildri," he answered.

I beamed. The name was perfect. A child of fire and peace that honored my father with part of his name. My perfect mate chose the perfect name. Would I ever stop falling in love with him more each day?

"It's perfect." My mother's elated voice came from behind me as she sat beside the Ice Queen.

"It is perfect," I agreed softly.

"Desildri. A perfect name for a perfect baby." I cooed at her beautiful face and twisted her little curls.

"I like it. Des for your father, and Ildri means fire and peace. Very smart." Dris scribbled against a small notepad on her lap for Emrys to read.

"Runira would have been nice but this is way better." My blood-worn goat Fae raised both of his thumbs. Nyx and Tor nodded.

"It is a strong name. A warrior in the making," the Ice Queen commented, and I grinned in her direction. She'd sent her ice phoenix back to their homeland. The weather here was too warm for long periods of time. The murmurs of Desildri's name calmed after a few minutes and everyone picked at their plates.

"When is everyone leaving?" I'd thought about this conversation earlier, and readied my heart for their answers.

"Two days." The Ice Queen spoke first. Rista had been working hard with her gifts to keep portals open for the dead to be transferred. She should be

247

done with that in about two days, so the queen's departure made sense. As much as I wanted more time with my new friends, they had kingdoms to run and loved ones to return to.

"I'm leaving in three," Kunsala answered softly. Dris placed a comforting arm over her shoulder.

"A week," Tor answered and bit back the sob.

I wasn't ready to part ways with him or Nyx. They meant too much to me, my closest friends. Despite the hold on my emotions, I knew they were written on my face. Nyx breathed deeply like she was trying to keep from crying, too. I feared if I opened my mouth, all my fears would tumble out. For the rest of the night, I refrained from talking too much.

Rune held me close while I tried to sleep and failed. Desildri slept deeply but would wake in the middle of the night to feed. My mind raced as I realized I'd become queen within the next two days. I knew that day would come but I didn't expect it so soon.

"Rune," I nudged, even though I felt bad for waking him up. He grumbled but his thumb moved idly against my stomach.

"Are you nervous about becoming king?" It went without saying that when I became queen, my husband would move up the royal scale with me.

"No." He yawned, and I almost laughed.

"I'm nervous."

"As long as you freshen your breath, you'll be fine." His grip tightened as I tried to roll away from him. The jerk teased me as I voiced my fears.

"Sapphira, you're already a leader and queen to your people, especially after all you've done for them. The only thing that will change is your title." He pressed a kiss to my head and I settled back into his warmth beneath the blanket. He fell asleep minutes after and I let what he said relax me. No matter what happened I would be the best queen I could be. And I had support to help fix my crown when it started to slip. Everything was gonna work out. I just needed to have faith.

Chapter Forty-Four

Dris

I signed to Emrys that it was time. He nodded, and I leaned over to kiss his cheek. During the battle, he'd tried to take down a giant and got knocked in the head. He had suffered a concussion which led to his hearing loss. Rista said he may get some back over time, but it wasn't guaranteed. We'd been learning sign language together over these last few days. Even our friends had joined in as much as they could, which I know meant so much to Emrys. Every day he found flowers for me to express himself, and I kept him talking to keep the muscle memory strong. He already knew how to read lips from his profession and I was forever grateful for that.

A crowd gathered in front of the ruins of the palace for the coronation. The queen stood beside Celestine, as Sapphira and Rune walked hand and hand down the aisle between the masses. This type of event was usually overdone with massive decorations and parties. However, our kingdom lacked in many of those things now. We did what we could and I don't think anyone truly cared. Sapphira and Rune wore fine clothes of white and silver. Both of their cloaks had the symbol of Crysia on the back—our proud tree with roots that wrapped downward to the hilt of a sword with a blade that pointed upward. We were a strong and proud people, even in the face of devastation.

Desildri screamed from Nyx's arms when her parents came into view. They beamed at their baby while Nyx rocked her. The woman was a natural mother. I suspected once Tor and she had settled into their new roles, they would be popping out a baby soon. Though I kept my suspicions to myself.

Our soon-to-be rulers knelt before my aunt Celestine as she blessed their reign. They vowed to protect Crysia and rule with strength of heart, protect the kingdom, and serve its people. The ceremony was short, without theatrics. Sapphira cried when her mother revealed a crown made of onyx, diamonds, and bits of sapphire. Her father had created it for her when she was younger in hopes that she would always carry a part of her family with her for as long as she reigned. Rune's crown was a mixture of onyx and tiger's eye. It was simple with a silver crescent moon on the front.

"I present to you, the people of Crysia and our honored guests, Queen Sapphira and King Rune." The two stood as Celestine announced them, and I clapped loudly for my friends. Sapphira wiped the tears from her cheeks and looked lovingly at her husband and king. They'd been through so much and grew into the full versions of themselves that they were always meant to be. Destiny led them through every heart break and adventure to this moment. Emrys's hand joined mine and I glanced at *my* mate, my partner in life.

"I love you." I signed it back to him for practice. We talked about our lives and what we wanted a lot recently. Rebuilding Crysia was our number one priority, but what came after?

Talks with Kunsula and time spent with my mischievous mate led me to crave new experiences. I wanted to travel, to see the places I read about, try new foods, and visit as many libraries as possible. Emrys supported this plan and proved to be my match in every way. He'd seen a lot of places in his life but wanted to see them again with me. A life shared together—that was our most precious dream.

"Hail, Queen Sapphira and King Rune," the crowd chanted, and everyone took turns congratulating the new rulers.

"Party time!" Emrys clapped his hands together. I shook my head but I truly loved everyone's smiles in this moment. So many tears of despair had been shed. We had much to build upon, much sadness to bear on our shoulders. Yet a new age had begun and its future was yet to be written.

The people of Crysia cheered and danced until the early morning hours. Sapphira's mom babysat while we drank and laughed into the next day. I'd started assisting our builders with plans for a new city. Since the slate had essentially been burned clean, Sapphira requested we build with a new design while remembering the principles we held dear. My special project was creating a new library for our people to use and learn new trades. With Verin gone and the Dramens nearly eradicated, Sapphira promised to open the portals and extend a hand to the surviving humans. They needed us, and we needed to be the keepers of balance and peace. People already felt safe to travel again with magic coursing through the world. Our city would stand as a beacon of hope to everyone who needed it. Human or Fae.

The days passed quickly, and we'd said our goodbyes to our allies. I hugged my new friend and promised to visit soon. The grief of Kunsula losing her brother hit hard, but instead of focusing on the pain every second, she chose to remember their bond. The happy times. As long as we remembered our loved ones that have moved on, they lived around us, in our essence and in our hearts.

The bittersweet farewells lasted days until the hardest of them all finally arrived. Tor and Nyx would travel with his mother back to their new home. Tor had only been sent to Crysia for one purpose—to marry

Sapphira. Of course it didn't work out that way in the end. Both had found their true mates and happiness. Now Tor had his own destiny to live out with Nyx alongside him. We'd spent so much time together and experienced so much that this particular goodbye ached. We all tried to show our joy because we were joyous for our friends who left to start their own grand adventure.

"Thank you for finding me and dragging me here." Sapphira embraced Tor tightly with tears on her cheeks. His lips pressed to her forehead then they separated.

"Who would have thought that smelly human girl would go on to save the world and become queen?" the prince teased, and Sapphira stuck out her tongue. It's hard to believe a few months ago Sapphira was a human survivor, and now she stood before us as our ruler.

"Definitely not me." Our queen laughed, as Nyx walked over to her and nudged her.

"I'll be coming to visit soon. Queen's promise." Sapphira hugged her oldest friend tightly. She'd already vowed that we'd have a girls' night, as soon as the citizens of Crysia weren't sleeping in tents anymore. Nyx's hand snuck out from their embrace and pulled me in.

"Take care, brother." Rune smacked a hand on Tor's shoulder, then pulled him into a hug. Change was hard, nobody really liked the transitional stages of life. But if we remained stagnant, we gave up the opportunities to become our highest self. Rune and Tor were full-fledged brothers now, in more ways than simply blood . . . a truly beautiful sight to see how their bond had grown. It was then as I watched those two men who fought their sibling bond, and embraced each other with smiles that I truly understood.

No matter how far apart we'd all be, no matter the trials we'd yet to face, we'd forever have each other. This moment of goodbyes hurt, and yes we were happy to have become a family. But this wasn't the end . . . our end. There would be more adventures and more talks over tea and wine together.

Our story was only getting started.

The End...

................Or is it?

Sapphira

"Too slow!" Rune growled, and I crouched before him with my sword ready.

"Seriously!" I lunged as he took a step closer, and my sword missed him by a mere inch. My body rolled on the grass, and a rock tore the leggings at my thigh.

"Can't you take it easy on me? I'm your queen," I whined even though it would spur Rune to train me harder.

"No."

"Have it your way then." I was done training for the day. Months after the war ended, Rune and I continued to work on my battle form. It was nice to train with him when we had time. Now that I ruled as queen, I refused to let my body and skill go soft. Our daughter would need us to fight for her and protect her as she grew into her powers.

"Come at me, highness." Rune smirked and I glanced at the waterfall we loved so much. Too bad I didn't have powers to manipulate the water beyond creating ice. I dropped my sword and pretended to gather my powers to strike. Rune narrowed his eyes, his feet dug into the earth a tiny bit more.

My hands gripped at the hem of my shirt and I pulled the material up to flash him. Distraction at its finest.

"Not gonna work this time." Rune chuckled and I jumped a little for the added effect. I was done training, but I could easily muster up the energy for another type of cardio.

"Sapphira..." My mate growled and I grinned with victory so close. Suddenly, the ground moved around my feet. My hands dropped my shirt as I tried to move but my feet were stuck. The ground rolled like a landslide straight to the water. The river's chill froze my arousal to where annoyance burned alone.

"Seriously?" I hollered and my mate stood at the edge of the water. His hands resting behind his head triumphantly. I swished my hand and the rock beneath his feet moved away. He slipped into the water beside me and I laughed so hard my stomach ached.

"Sneaky little queen." His wet hand caressed my cheek and that arousal melted into a fiery blaze again. My king stared into me before his lips pressed to my nose.

"Grumpy old king."

"A grumpy king and a sneaky queen, together endlessly," he muttered before his hands lifted me up to straddle his lap in the water.

"Old." He pulled back to scoff, eyes filled with mischief. I kissed his neck then turned our training session into a mission of utmost importance. Getting him to show me what those old man hips could do until the end of our immortal days.

Well, at least until we needed to relieve the babysitter.

THE REAL END THIS TIME.

For now . . .

Sapphira and her squad's story is over. But I can think of someone else from this world with a big destiny that surely has a story to tell. Can't you ;)

Pre-Order Available-Click here

 Click here to be notified first about the updates on the continuation of the saga.

More Books by Jessica Florence

https://www.jessicaflorenceauthor.com/books

To go Directly to Amazon click here.

Dawn (Hero Society #1)

Dawn has come, a time for heroes to rise. Draco has lived long and felt the pain of loss more than anyone in one lifetime could imagine.

Immortality was given to him as a gift, a gift that failed him and turned him into a shell of the man that has nothing left but to wait out the end of existence alone.

Until her.

Rose is an empath who sees more than who Draco is supposed to be: she sees him, and what they could be. Together, they will begin the search for others with extraordinary powers, to stop a war that's been brewing for over a millennia.

The journey is only beginning, and an unnamed enemy has started to make his mark on their world.

The dawn of heroes has finally arrived.

Only time will tell if it's too late to defeat the upcoming darkness of night that now descends upon all of mankind.

Weighing of the Heart

What happens when the myths of old become reality?

Thalia Alexander has lived her life in peace until her twenty-fifth birthday when she has a strange dream about a man.

A tall, dark, and sexy man that shows up at her work the next morning.

Tristan Jacks is trouble with a capital T, but for some strange reason she is drawn to him like nothing she has ever experienced before. He has this possessiveness and adoration for her that she can't explain. It's like they have known each other forever.

Thalia's strange dreams continue to stalk her as her relationship with Tristan builds to be a love that will last the ages.

And when those dreams and reality start to clash, will Thalia be able to handle the truth?

Could the world of ancient myths truly exist in modern times?

The Final KO

I fight for a living.

Which makes finding a decent guy hard when you're a female MMA fighter. None of them have been my equal. I yearn for a man who can push me to reach new heights and challenge me. A man who will treat me like a lady then lift me up by my ass and impale me against the wall.

But when Arson Kade, MMA's top fighter and notorious manwhore, declares he's that man for me I have my doubts. Any sane woman would.

There seems to be more to Arson than the rumors that surround him, but will it make me fall hard or run for the hills?
I know I've got no choice but to hold on for the ride.

It's the main event and my heart's on the line.
But will it be the Final KO?

The Final Chase

 I never thought one day I'd make a bet about pedicures to a man and loose.

But of course, I'd never man like him.
Jake Wild. Owner of Wild rescue for exotic animals.
He's everything I'm not, my polar opposite.
I'm heels and my salon,
He's dirt and his creatures.
But much like the animals he cares for, he's got that carnal edge.
He's the type of man you crawl on your hands and knees for.
He bites, he's on the hunt, and now I'm his prey
A chance meeting and a bet started the undeniable attraction between us.
But I'm not giving my heart and soul away that easy, he's going to have to catch me first.
It's the ultimate game of cat and mouse,
But will it be our Final Chase?

Long Drive

There is a long road in everyone's journey in life.
For some people, it's a way to get from one place to another.
For others, it's a search for one's purpose in existence.
For me, the road was where I could find peace.
When everything in my life had shattered, I turned to the road.
And that's where I met him.
Killian Lemarque.
A beautiful truck driver, and my salvation.
One month on the road together is the deal, and when it's over, I will have hopefully figured out what I'm going to do about my torn reality.
But sometimes the road can change everything.
Falling in love wasn't part of my plan nor his.

But here we are.
One Month. One Truck. One Long Drive.

How You Get The Girl

As Hollywood's hottest actor, getting a woman in my bed is never a challenge.

But after seeing a feisty woman in bar who was looking for a one-night stand, I knew that her being in my bed wouldn't be enough.

She turned me down, and I thought I'd never see her again.

Fate had other plans though.

Alessandra Rose is now my lead makeup artist for the next four months. Literally, her job is to touch me every day for the duration of filming. Sounds like a win, right?

Nope, she stops me at every hint of a flirt. I'm in uncharted waters for once.

Her argument is good I'll give her that. I'm a good actor, so accepting that it's not all an act would be tough.

But I'm not going anywhere; here heart is my Grammy and him here to win it.

That's how you get the girl.

INSPIRED

Call it pure desperation, or maybe we'd agree it was the lack of sleep that had me signing six weeks of my life away to be bossed around by a life coach. Either way, I was trying to get my life together, and Logan Woodland was going to help.

I thought he'd make me eat healthier, drink more water, and do yoga. What I wasn't expecting, was to be forced to see myself as I was and how far I'd fallen.

But then his program worked.

He'd shown me a life filled with passion and desire. A life where I was stronger and could be the woman I'd never known existed inside me.

I did have a six-week life-changing experience, but now, I wanted more than I'd signed on for.

Him.

Guiding Lights

He sings of suffering. His eyes hold the pain of living
in sorrow.
The moment our gaze meets recognition flares
within.
We are tortured souls drifting in a sea of darkness.
He knows I have secrets that I'll never tell.
I am numb.
I am broken.
I can never be the guiding light through the
darkness he thinks I am.
I have forsaken my past, I rely on keeping myself
shut off.
I wish things were different, that maybe we could
be each other's lifeline.
But destiny drags us down like an anchor.
He lives his life in the lime light of a famous rock
star, and I live in shadows on the run.

I wished I'd known that before I fell for him, but
now it's too late.

Blinding Lights

She dances with a passion I'll never know.
Seeing her again tears me at the seams.
She was never mine.
My soul is stained with the darkness of death.
I have killed.
I have tortured.
I have lost.
Her soul is too bright for the shadows I live in
and her determination to be the flame in my heart
could kill us both.
Still, I want her, I crave her.
But not even her blinding lights can fight away the
darkness threatening us both.

But I refuse to lose her, and this time I don't think I
can walk away.

Evergreen

It was supposed to be an easy stakeout.
Until a bunch of bachelorettes mobbed me,
changing my life forever.

I couldn't get Andi Slaton, with her red hair, blue
eyes, and cotton candy-flavored lip gloss, out of my
head.

But when she offers herself to aid the FBI to help
me take down the biggest criminal family in Tampa,
Florida, my very sanity is put to the test watching
her spend time with my arch enemy.

She's everything I want, I will be everything to her.
We will be Evergreen.

Acknowledgments

It's crazy to think Sapphira's story is done. This trilogy has changed my life in so many ways and I have you all to thank for it.

Every reader, both new and Jflo seasoned, you guys are everything. Thank you for giving me a try.

To my beta/alpha readers. Christina, Salina, Nikki, Autumn, Krystal, Emily, Tina, and Melissa... I couldn't have written without your help and feedback.

To my author buds, thank you for inspiring me and helping fix my crown when it slipped. I appreciate you guys so much.

To the bloggers, and bookstagrammers that help promote my stories. I love you guys. You are the mac to my cheese.

Lorraine, as always you help turn my beautiful book into something epic with your editing.

Virginia, lawd I don't know what I'd do without you.

Sarah... YOU GODDESS YOU. This cover was amazing.. AH-MAZING.

Husband, I love you, you sweet and growling jackass.

Kiddo, you inspire me and I love watching you become your own person. You keep my imagination fresh and young. <3

About the Author

Jessica Florence writes the stories that her fellow nerds
yearn for.

From Superheroes to Sexy Truckers, Jessica is known to
give readers unique tales of hope where love conquers
all. Stories that melt away reality and take you on a
journey with the characters. If escapism is what you are
looking for, then look no further. Jessica is the Queen of
weaving the tales you may not normally pick up but find
yourself not being able to put down.

Jessica's always had a love of reading, and her love of
books lead her to start writing in the 9th grade. She
quickly learned that storytelling was her passion.
Inspired by movies, music, and her personal life she
writes like it's the very air she breathes. Through her
writing it's evident that she lives for the stories she
creates.

Jessica grew up in North Carolina, and currently resides
in Southwest Florida with her daughter, husband, and
German Shepherd. She loves to be outside, write in her
hammock, and collect tea mugs.

CONNECT WITH J-FLO:

→ FACEBOOK: facebook.com/jessicaflorenceauthor →
INSTAGRAM: Instagram.com/authorjessicaflorence →
TWITTER: twitter.com/@Florence_jess → PINTEREST:

Made in the USA
Monee, IL
15 May 2021